Bold Seduction
(Of Professor Hornsby)

The Hornsby Brothers #1

By

Karyn Gerrard

Table of Contents

Bold Seduction (Of Professor Hornsby)

Copyright © 2015, 2019 by Karyn Gerrard

KG Publishing

Vers 2.2

PRINT ISBN: 978-1-7386845-3-3

Cover art by © The Write Designer

The Hornsby Brothers Series

THREE BROTHERS, THE sons of the Duke of Gransford, are diverse in their natures, and so are their choices when it comes to love. Growing up in a loving household, each is determined to seek true love. Searching for it, however, is different from finding and leads each of the brothers to unlikely places and chance encounters with what society would consider unsuitable women.

BOOK ONE IS *Bold Seduction (of Professor Hornsby)* and concerns the youngest son, Spencer Hornsby.

Book two is *The Vicar's Frozen Heart* and concerns the middle son, Tremain Hornsby.

Book three, *The Marquess of Secrets,* concerns the oldest son and heir to the duke, Harrison Hornsby, the Marquess of Tennington.

Author's Note

CONCERNING THE YOUNGEST Hornsby brother, Spencer: If diagnosed today, Spencer would fall on the spectrum of a mild form of autism. In the Victorian era, there were a few recorded accounts of children manifesting similar aspects. Back then, they were usually diagnosed with "children's psychosis" and taken to the asylum.

As far as epilogues go, I generally don't use them in every book, I did add a short one here, and you will find one in the third and final book of this series, *The Marquess of Secrets*, where you can catch up with the brothers and how their loves and lives progressed.

Bold Seduction was previously published with Kensington/Lyrical Press in 2015. This revised, re-edited version has over 10,000 additional words.

Characters from my historical romance novels mentioned and/or appearing in this story:

Gideon Broyles, The Duke of Watford. The Duke of Pain (The Rakes of St. Regent's Park #4)

Tremain Hornsby. The Vicar's Frozen Heart (The Hornsby Brothers #2)

Harrison Hornsby, the Marquess of Tennington. The Marquess of Secrets (The Hornsby Brothers #3)

Summary

A FASCINATING PROPOSITION

As the owner of the Starling Club, one of London's more popular brothels, Philomena McGrattan has seen and heard it all. There is little that surprises her anymore and even less that interests her. When she is presented with an opportunity for a tempting and bold seduction, she can't help but rise to the challenge. A virgin son of a duke? How could she refuse?

An Improbable Encounter

Quiet and set in his ways, Lord Spencer Hornsby is a brilliant eccentric who prefers solitude and researching ancient civilizations. Alone in the Welsh countryside, with only his two wolfhounds for company, Spencer has little time or patience for the pleasures of society. But when an unexpected guest arrives at his isolated hunting lodge, Spencer cannot help but be irresistibly intrigued by the presence of this beautiful woman.

Philomena is shocked to discover that the odd professor stirs up feelings she thought long dead. Spencer, ever the man of research, is eager to learn all he can. Will they find deeper emotions are in play as they take their journey of discovery?

Prologue

PHILOMENA MCGRATTAN, madam and owner of the Starling Club brothel, thought she'd heard everything. However, this unexpected request managed to intrigue her.

"Is this a joke? A planned humiliation for this supposed friend of yours? I will not allow any of my girls to be used in such a manner." She narrowed her gaze, studying the two men sitting opposite.

They shook their heads vigorously. The dark-haired one—what *was* his name—gave her a determined look.

"Not at all," he replied. "We admire Spence; we would never disgrace or embarrass him. Your brothel was highly recommended; the ladies are presentable and experienced by all accounts. Spence, or rather, Lord Spencer Hornsby, will soon celebrate his thirtieth birthday—not that he celebrates much of anything—and we thought to give him a surprise gift: a night with a woman who would be kind and patient but knowledgeable in the carnal arts. You see, Spence is...well...." The man coughed and glanced down at his hands while the other gentleman, a ginger-haired bloke named Jacob, nodded.

"Spence is the third son of the Duke of Gransford," Jacob interjected, picking up the narrative. "Spence is a rather eccentric chap who prefers to be called Professor Hornsby rather than Lord Hornsby.

Spence lives a solitary life buried in research and academia. Has for years. He's never been with a woman. Never kissed one either, as far as I am aware."

How fascinating. A male virgin of aristocratic birth.

Granted, a third son of a duke may not have a title of his own, but he did have the use of the courtesy style of "Lord." This would be quite a feather in her brothel's cap. It could open up a whole new breed of customer—virgin sons of the aristocracy—though surely the list must be small. Such a list may even be non-existent, considering the wicked reputations of most in the peerage.

The Duke of Gransford.

Phil tapped her chin thoughtfully. She'd heard of him—and the family. A favorite of the queen, at least according to the papers. Champions of the poor. Not that His Grace ever darkened her door. Perhaps one of his sons? No, she would have remembered, for she always made notations of any aristocrat customers in her ledger.

"Rich beyond measure."

She remembered that quote regarding the family from a recent newspaper article. Perhaps she could add a surcharge on the virgin professor. A goodly amount seeing he was wealthy.

With a soft "hmm," Phil moved from tapping her chin to drumming her fingers on the desk as she mulled over the golden opportunity before her. Were these men genuine? Or perhaps they were acting concerned for their friend to convince her to go along with the scheme—all for the express purpose of degrading the shy professor.

Life may have turned her bitter and cynical, but Phil would never participate in such a mortifying plan. Sex should not be used as a weapon, especially toward a studious celibate with no experience. It would be unimaginably cruel.

"If I were to agree, this enterprise would *not* be cheap. I will require a fifty percent payment up front." Standing, she braced her hands on the desk and leaned forward. "Where does this hermit professor-lord live? If the distance is far, you'll pay for transportation as well. Will your Lord Hornsby turn away the girl I send? Is he amenable to such an arrangement? Has he mentioned that he wishes to be rid of his virginity? Some would not appreciate a 'surprise' of this nature."

The two men exchanged dubious looks. "He *is* a man," Jacob shrugged. "Once the prostitute...I mean...young lady makes her intentions clear; I cannot see why he would *not* be agreeable. Spence lives like a monk in that damned crumbling castle-like hunting manor—"

From her standing position, Phil observed the dark-haired man kicking Jacob in the shin, quickly silencing him.

A challenge. How fascinating. And perhaps one I will personally take on.

The money is quite the inducement.

Already her mind added up the various expenses, surcharges, and other fees. As far as she could ascertain, the men appeared to be telling the truth. A little investigation into this proposal was undoubtedly in order.

Phil made up her mind. Best to snatch up a lucky happenstance when it presents itself.

Yes, a golden opportunity indeed.

"Gentlemen, we have a deal—pending certain particulars and background checks regarding all the parties involved. My club will take on the assignment."

Chapter 1

LATE DECEMBER 1881
Wales

AFTER AN AGONIZING six-and-a-half-hour train ride from London to Tenby, Wales, Phil sat in an open cart heading toward the residence of Professor Lord Hornsby, or whatever he wished to be called. Phil would never recover from the discomfort she'd been exposed to.

The train ride took forever, seemingly stopping at every town and village along the route. As far as comfort, she might as well have ridden in the baggage car, for she had been bounced around like a battered piece of luggage. Now she was being jostled about in a wagon—the indignity of it all.

Ultimately, Phil decided to take on the professor-virgin mission herself. At thirty-three years of age, she concluded she would be the only one with the fortitude, comprehension, and patience needed for such a delicate job. The seduction must be subtle, and if he refuses the gift from his friends? All the better. All she needed to do was collect her payment and return to London immediately.

Boredom and restlessness had settled into her life over the past several years. Phil longed to escape the everyday running of the brothel, even if it was temporary. Truthfully speaking, she wanted the money all to herself as there was a future to plan for. *Her* future. The third son of a prominent, wealthy duke would be able to pay—and pay well. Perhaps a surcharge *and* a gratuity.

How greedy. But she must think of her own needs.

What if he refused to pay? Or what if his lordship was a secret murderer? Lured to a remote spot, it would be easy to remove her permanently and bury her remains in some desolate section of his rambling property. It's obvious she read too many murder mysteries and magazines focusing on true crime.

Smiling slightly, Phil touched her leg. Strapped to her upper thigh was a small knife in a leather holder, which she had never used—the first time for everything. There were enough sleepless nights this week as she prepared for her journey. Trepidation, to be specific. Could this be a setup? With her as the victim? Was unbridled voracity leading her into a trap? Taking on any outside assignment was a risk, not one she or her girls usually considered.

Over the years, Phil became skilled in assessing a person's character, and as far as she could tell, the gentlemen who hired her were in earnest. And they checked out. Darius Brownlow, her resident protector and assistant, reported that the men were legitimate and that the duke's youngest son was called Spencer and considered harmless, albeit an eccentric hermit. Maybe she should have brought Darius with her as security. Being an ex-boxer, his physical presence was formidable. However, he was needed at the club.

Too late now. Enough thinking of money or any possible perilous situations.

Completing the job must come first. If she ever got there. What happened to the sun? The clouds were rather ominous. Hopefully, she would arrive at her destination before it rained or snowed. Her mind pinged from one thought to another, which proved her anxiety.

"Are we there yet? How long will it take?" Phil cried to the driver, trying to be heard above the clopping of the horses' hooves and the increasingly loud wind gusts.

"Another hour, missy. His lordship lives apiece."

Another hour?

A swift exit may not be possible. How awkward and inconvenient.

"What are all these packages?" she asked.

The small wagon overflowed with numerous parcels and boxes wrapped in brown paper.

"'Tis his lordship's food order. I come up this way but once every six or seven days."

What? Once a week? Surely, I misheard him.

A feeling of foreboding took hold. "You must be mistaken. I'm only staying two nights." Or no nights at all. Phil grabbed her bonnet to keep a brisk blast of air from carrying it away.

"Unless you made other arrangements, missy, this be the only transport to his lordship's. Once a week. I know for a fact that Lord Hornsby don't keep horses and coaches and the like."

Phil will *slay* those two popinjays who hired her. They never once mentioned that salient piece of information.

Drat it.

She should've asked for more details regarding the location and transport. Now she would be stuck at the virgin professor's hovel for close to a blasted week! Anger boiled her blood to a dangerously high heat level.

The two men who had hired her also cheapened out on the transportation. They paid third class for her train journey, leaving her to sit on a hard-wooden bench the entire distance. What an insult. Now she was being bounced about in a bloody merchant's wagon. Her cheeks flushed in annoyance. Phil had assumed a private carriage would pick her up at the train station. What a shock to discover the open-air utility wagon was only fit for hauling machine parts or lumber.

What should she do? Turn around and make the return trip with the grizzled grocer? What a complete waste of her time.

"What does the professor do in an emergency? If a doctor was needed, how would he fetch one? What sane man would live in such a circumstance?"

The driver shrugged. "Beats me, missy. He be a strange one."

Phil exhaled. It would be foolish to travel all this way just to turn around and depart. Besides, she could not abide another train ride back to London on the same day if it could be managed. Probably not, which meant staying at an inn in Tenby.

Meals. More expense.

"I'll pay you extra to return in two days," she offered the old man hopefully.

There goes part of my profit.

He shook his head as he puffed on his pipe. "Nay. I be a busy man. I don't make trips here with an empty wagon. Stick to me schedule; I do. I've other customers besides his lordship."

Phil gritted her teeth in exasperation. Christmas came and went the previous week, but she did not feel particularly festive. Sitting behind her were two small pieces of luggage packed with enough clothes for two days. She would've tossed in more woolens if Phil knew it would be this bloody cold.

Shivering, she pulled her shawl close about her shoulders. The bracing breeze chilled her bones. Not even the sun made an appearance to warm her. Glancing at her surroundings, Phil noticed the scenery had turned bleak and sparse. A barren landscape free of humans and cottages trailed behind her for several miles as the driver continued on his path.

An uneasiness took hold again. This could be one of the biggest blunders of her life. Considering what mistakes she had made already, what was one more to add to the list?

After an eternity, the wagon turned up a full-of-ruts narrow and twisting road. Trees closed in; the leafless branches scraped together in the wind making a mournful sound that complimented the austere scenery.

A crumbling residence came into view. It was certainly significant for a hunting lodge. Granted, one of the men referred to it as castle-like. Though the structure was perched on the edge of a cliff, she would hardly describe it as a castle as the place lacked medieval grandeur. However, the black stone structure was foreboding and ancient. The property was surrounded by a wrought iron fence that leaned in all directions from apparent neglect. A small garden area, if it could be called that, was choked off by a tangle of weeds.

Pulling the wagon to the rear entrance, the older man halted the horses and jumped down. "You best come in this way, missy. No one to greet you at the front." The grocer grabbed a few parcels and made his way toward the door.

Phil shook her head in disbelief as she gingerly descended from the wagon. Over to the side of the property was a small barn structure, no doubt for the absent horses. She collected her two small carpetbags and followed the driver through the servants' entrance.

An older woman sat at a rickety table drinking from a jar. Her feet were propped up, her stockings bunched at the ankles. Tangles of wiry gray hair poked outward under her dirty lace cap, and her faded wool gown sported a tattered hem. The apron that covered her garments contained stains of dubious origins.

"Thanks be to God ye made it. We be runnin' low of foodstuffs, William. Thought I'd have to dig for roots in the ground to gnaw on!" The woman cackled at her joke. She sobered when her gaze fell upon Phil. "Who be this? His nibs ain't expectin' company." The woman's bloodshot eyes scanned Phil thoroughly. "She be a tart. Look at the paint on her face and the fancy dress."

William laid the parcels on the table and shrugged. "Came from London on the train. She knew where to find me and waved papers with his lordship's name and directions to this place right under me nose."

"Excuse me? I'm standing right here," Phil said, annoyance lacing her tone.

"Aye, I see ye standin' there and all. I'll not stay and wait on a doxy. Who sent ye? His nibs wouldn't. Don't even know what a woman looks like; I'll be bound."

The older woman coughed and spat on the floor. Phil winced. The kitchen was an abomination. Cobwebs clung stubbornly to every nook and cranny. Dirty crockery sat in a sink, and used pots were piled on the stove. Garbage and rotting food littered the floor. The surroundings fit the woman's filthy appearance.

"Can someone escort me to Lord Hornsby?" Phil asked, trying not to wrinkle her nose in disgust.

"William! Don't unload the gin! I be comin' back with ye." The servant stood and reached for her valise.

"Wait, where are you going? Where are the servants?" Phil cried.

"I be it and be damned if I'll stay here with a trollop. Ye are one; I can see it. Tell his nibs I quit and to send me wages with the next wagon."

William continued his trek of bringing in the packages and boxes. How dare the old harridan leave her alone in this mess—and with a strange man? The reference to being a trollop and a doxy stung, though she should be used to it by now. It must be tattooed on her forehead. Regardless, unease picked at her insides. Then a flash of anger replaced her discomfort and hurt.

"Then leave, old woman. As housekeepers go, you're sadly lacking. I can smell the liquor on you. Never have I seen a more disorganized and grimy working area," Phil sniffed with disdain.

The woman blanched, narrowing her gaze and clearly showing her contempt. "How dare ye talk to me in such a way? Uppity prossie." She stomped out of the kitchen.

William seemingly ignored the whole drama and piled the packages on the table. After one last trip, he turned to face her.

"This be your last chance. Won't be back for about a week, weather willing. Are you coming?"

Sharing the cramped wagon with that filthy, smelly housekeeper churned her guts. Her stubbornness prevailed.

"No, I'll stay. See you in six days."

William shrugged and closed the door behind him. Phil stood in the grubby kitchen and listened to the sound of the horses and wagon as they disappeared.

What have I done? I am well and truly stuck.

No use fulminating over this, she thought. Might as well head upstairs and make her introductions. Phil placed her bags on a bare spot on the counter. She removed her wool coat, shawl, gloves, and bonnet. At least a roaring fire crackled in the hearth, warming the space.

After locating the backstairs, Phil took a deep breath and climbed.

God knows what manner of man would greet her.

Chapter 2

PHIL HAD A FONDNESS for reading Gothic novels. She brought a copy of Elizabeth Gaskell's *The Doom of the Griffiths* with her. She had never dreamed of finding herself in a Gothic setting, but here she stood.

The hallways were dark and narrow, which made traversing difficult. Everything smelled of dampness and decay. The lighting in the place consisted of a strange combination of candelabras and oil lamps, which showed how new mixed with old. Considering the isolation, Phil would hazard to guess there was no gas lighting here. With each step she took, the floor groaned and squeaked in response. A light flickered from under the door at the end of the long hallway. The sound of barking dogs startled her enough that she nearly jumped out of her skin.

"Justinian, Theodora, quiet!"

Phil stopped dead in her tracks at the deep, commanding voice. The animals were immediately silenced. Who wouldn't at such an authoritative tone? Taking a calming breath, she knocked on the door. There was no response. Sighing, she tried again. Nothing.

To hell with it.

Phil turned the handle and crossed the threshold. What immediately struck her was the coziness. A fire blazed in a stone hearth on the left side of the room. Before it laid two large gray dogs the size of ponies. They eyed her with indifference, but a keen intelligence shone in their gazes—which they kept firmly on her. What were the beasts, wolfhounds? Enough speculation on the dogs. Phil turned toward the ornate desk at the front of the room and the man sitting behind it.

The professor sat hunched over, his pen scratching furiously. He was a great hairy man with nary an inch of skin showing through. His long wavy locks, which hung forward like a pair of curtains, contained a varied mix of light and dark shades of brown. Immersed in his work, he didn't look up or acknowledge her presence. How rude. But typical, she imagined, for the son of a duke. To those of the upper class, everyone below them barely existed.

Waiting for any acknowledgment, Phil inspected the room more closely. Bookcases stuffed with ancient tomes filled every wall. On either side of the desk were two tables, the surface covered with books, maps, and scrolls, topped off with dust. No doubt the man himself would smell as musty as this room, dust and cobwebs collecting on his shoulders.

"You may leave the tray, Mrs. Brickell."

Phil paused momentarily to allow his voice's sultry and deep rumbling tone to seep into her being. The sound lingered and made her weak in the knees—quite a surprise since most men didn't garner any response from her at all. Though cultured and refined, his voice held a confident, sultry—purr. Yes, that was the word that described it.

Enough, Phil. Focus.

Be damned if she would speak. She wanted to see how long it would take before he looked up and saw that she wasn't the grubby housekeeper.

The professor stopped writing, flipped through a stack of papers, stroked his beard, glanced at the nearby bookcase, and muttered a quiet "oh." He rose from his chair, and the loud creak accompanying his movement meant the source to be either the banker's chair or the professor. Shock moved through her upon seeing him lurch toward the bookcase to retrieve a stack of yellowed parchment, keeping the same bent posture he had while sitting.

Bloody hell, is the man a cripple?

Not that it matters.

But it was yet another significant fact those idiots neglected to mention. She shook the surprising revelation from her mind. The professor then moved swiftly to his chair and sat with the same crooked stance. Another disturbing creak could be heard, and she exhaled in relief once she discovered the sound came from the oak chair. The poor man had a physical impediment. Not crucial to the job at hand as Phil was paid to do a job regardless of the customer's various hindrances.

Obviously, he was not going to address her presence, so she cleared her throat and said, "If you're referring to that drunk, putrid old woman lurking about your filthy kitchen, I regret to inform you she's done a runner."

The professor laid his pen on the desk, slowly lifted his head, cocked his thick eyebrows, and gazed at her. "Indeed?"

As she surmised, a great hairy beast sat before her. His unruly hair stuck out in all directions as if it hadn't been combed in many days. He stared at her with great owl eyes. His spectacles were huge, taking up half his face, while the other half was covered in a bushy beard of all shades of color. She wouldn't be surprised to find a swallow making a nest in it.

The brief attraction she experienced at hearing his provocative voice dissipated like a morning fog. This man resembled one of the grimy beggars frequenting the streets of London.

A duke's son? Impossible.

Finally, he asked, "And who are you, her replacement?"

Should I pretend to be a servant? A housekeeper? Bugger that.

"Hardly. I believe the old hag planned to leave anyway since her bag was packed and ready. I'm here at the invitation of two of your acquaintances. Mr. Jacob Williamson and Mr. Clive Christopher."

The professor frowned. At least, she thought he did. It was hard to read his expression under the wiry thatch of hair surrounding his mouth. He rifled through a pile of unopened correspondence.

"I do not recall any recent note from those gentlemen."

"You *are* Professor Hornsby? Third son of the Duke of Gransford?"

"I am."

"Well, my lord-professor, I believe I'm to be a surprise present for your birthday tomorrow."

His owl eyes blinked rapidly as if he couldn't process what she said. "I do not require a maid, though you tell me Mrs. Brickell has departed. It appears I could use a housekeeper...."

The professor had absolutely no idea why she came. His mind did not even consider that it could be for carnal reasons. What a sheltered life he must lead.

"I'm no servant, though you need tidying up as much as your house does. You bear a striking resemblance to a painting of a French-Canadian fur trapper I saw in a book once. All wild and shaggy—all that is missing is the plaid coat and the beaver pelts." She gave him her best sweet but counterfeit smile.

With his lips pressed into a straight line, he sat back and regarded her. "Oh? You read a book once?" His elegant voice dripped with self-righteous sarcasm.

"Touché, Professor. Well aimed. A direct hit." Phil pointed to the dogs, who still stared at her. Their unblinking attention followed her every minute move. "Should I be afeared for my life? Your animals *are* intimidating."

"Justinian. Theodora. Easy." The hounds relaxed at his command, resting their heads on their paws. "They're Irish Wolfhounds. 'Gentle when stroked, fierce when provoked.'"

Phil placed a hand on her hip. "Does that saying apply to you as well, Professor Hornsby?"

Did he smile slightly? Again, it was hard to tell under the facial hair. Phil pulled a chair toward the desk and placed it a few feet away. She raised one leg to the chair.

"I don't claim to be a blue-stocking, but I *can* read." With a deliberate movement, Phil grasped the hem of her green-striped gown and pulled it past her ankle boots. She glanced at the bewhiskered beast behind the desk. His gaze slid toward the raising of her petticoats to reveal one of her shapely legs. At least she'd been told they were shapely. Running her hand along the sheer white stocking, she lingered near her silk garter, careful not to expose the hidden knife.

"I don't think they're blue. The stockings, that is. You had better come closer and inspect their shade, Professor."

Coughing, he looked away. His gaze wandered, only resting on her twice since she entered the room. And he was doing it again, looking at everything *but* her. Phil would wager to guess she made him uncomfortable and—a little aroused. No sound could be heard except a whimper from one of the dogs and the massive clock in the corner ticking away the awkward minutes.

Hornsby's gaze, at last, rested on her. "Who *are* you, madam, and why are you here?"

She continued to fondle and caress her leg, and having the unkempt man watch her caused a slow roll of heat to travel through her. Again, his voice affected her like a cello played by a master that vibrated with life, power, and resonance.

"My name is Philomena McGrattan. I am indeed a madam, and I was hired to relieve you of your virginity."

There was no further reaction from the professor whatsoever. He didn't even blink.

This did not bode well.

At. All.

Chapter 3

OF ALL THE REPLIES this strange woman could give, that one Spencer did not expect. Damn, his interfering friends. The last time he'd been in their ignominious company, they teased him mercilessly about his virgin state. Never should have admitted to such a confidence, but he had imbibed in one too many brandies, and his tongue loosened.

They merely commented that the state should be taken care of soon. The teasing, he supposed, could be considered good-natured; it wasn't cruel, at least, as far as he could tell. He learned to ascertain the difference—in most cases.

Another acquaintance from university, Gideon Broyles, the Duke of Watford, recently invited him to join an exclusive club based in Regent's Park, where debauched adventures ruled the day. Gideon said it would assist with his social awkwardness. Spencer had wanted no part of it. Why would he? Was Gideon in on this farce as well? Perhaps, but he didn't remember the duke as being all that cruel or having any tolerance for pranks. It had been a while since he corresponded with any of his chums, Gideon included. Not that they were all that close, at least not of late. Not that he had that many chums to begin with.

Trying to make friends during his early school years came at the suggestion of his two older brothers, Harrison and Tremain. The process proved difficult, but he had discovered a few lads that could overlook particular idiosyncrasies of his personality. The trust built over a period of years, but Spencer always kept a part of himself removed from any interactions with others, even his family.

Perhaps he should have withdrawn from society altogether—and far sooner.

A slow simmer of anger stirred inside him. Were his so-called comrades lounging about at this club in London, laughing with smug satisfaction at their joke? Sending a woman for hire all this way to bed him? Spence's gaze narrowed. Perhaps this tart was in on it. Did this planned, malicious charade hurt him? No, that would come later when he was alone.

Miss McGrattan made for quite a vision, stroking her rather lovely leg. A ripple of desire caused his dormant prick to twitch slightly. Her gown, though garish, showed a certain style. The madam had an attractive figure and a pretty face. Her golden-red hair shimmered and glowed with health and vitality.

Is my birthday tomorrow?

Thinking about it, he ate turkey for dinner last week. At least he assumed it was turkey. The meat was as dry as a bone and rather tasteless. It meant that Christmas had come and gone for another year.

Back to the matter at hand.

"Please remove your limb from the chair, Madam McGrattan, and take a seat."

Giving him a brief pout, she sat, clasping her hands in her lap.

"I'm not sure what manner of payment my acquaintances promised for carrying out this means of humiliating me, but I will match the amount if you leave me alone."

She arched an eyebrow. "In the first place, Professor, your *friends* were genuinely concerned for your isolated state. This is *not* a joke at your expense, nor would I participate in someone's mortification. Second, I'm stuck here for the week. Under the circumstances, we can hardly avoid each other. If you're under the impression that I'll be bringing in trays of food to you or looking after your great beasts, you're bloody well mistaken."

Justinian woofed, raised his shaggy head, then rested it on his front paws, ignoring them both.

Her light brown eyes shone with determination—quite a striking shade, he mused, like tea after the milk had been added. A rush of relief washed through him at the declaration that his friends were not out to humiliate him. Miss McGrattan placed emphasis on the word 'friends,' and she spoke in a sincere manner; he would accept it as truth.

"We *will* be negotiating an additional amount for my inconvenience," she continued. "Your friends neglected to state that transport is only available every six or seven days. There may be other charges as well."

"I believe they were unaware of the transportation arrangements I have."

Miss McGrattan snorted.

One week.

The place was large enough that they could manage to avoid each other. Sharing accommodations with a stranger would upset his equilibrium; however, he must make an effort to keep his anxieties hidden. Spencer would pay whatever amount she demanded to stay clear of him. And when it came down to it, he couldn't very well turn her out into the teeth of winter weather.

"Hello? Did you hear me about the additional expenses?" she asked, her voice rising in annoyance.

"How can I help but hear you?" Spencer murmured. More loudly, he said, "On the second floor, there is a selection of rooms. Pick one of the least dusty ones, and there you may stay until William Boyle returns with the wagon in a week. We will discuss your varied and numerous fees later."

The madam crossed her arms across her ample chest, and the enticing glimpse of the swell of her bosom caused his shaft to twitch once again.

When conversing with people, he seldom made direct eye contact, often having to remind himself to act interested in what the other person was saying. Spencer didn't have to do it here. Miss McGrattan kept him focused, his gaze, for the most part, staying firmly on her.

"No, we'll discuss it here and now. I can see to the meals as I can cook, which will be one of the additional fees. You will eat in the bloody dining room with me. As I said, be damned if I'll wait on you. You do have one?"

"A dining room? Yes. Though it hasn't been used of late. Is your verbosity always this colorful?" Spencer asked.

"Many men like it. Yes, I suppose my talk could be considered salty."

"Much like your cooking, I'll wager to guess," he murmured.

The lady smiled, and the warmth of it caused his heart to tumble. "I like a man who gives as good as he gets. It bodes well for the task ahead."

"There will be no 'task' between us, Miss McGrattan."

She stood, smoothing her gown, which called attention to her shapely form. Spencer tried not to focus on the movement of her hands, but it proved futile.

"We'll see on that score. I always follow a job through. The additional fees?"

Money.

The reason she was here.

Spencer would do well to remember it. He had no idea what fees she was speaking of. What did he pay his housekeeper? About three pounds a month—an unheard-of sum—but the extra was for the isolation of the hunting lodge and for leaving him in peace. The older woman no doubt padded the grocery bill and pocketed the difference, but he didn't care as long as she left him alone.

He cleared his throat. "I will pay you twenty pounds for the week. You provide meals, and the rest of the time, stay out of my sight."

"Make it sixty. I'm losing income being here for the week. And the hardship. And the location and inadequate travel arrangements. And lack of proper accommodations. Your place, Professor, is a sty suitable for farm animals."

"Sty?"

"A dump, a hovel, a shack, a dirty place. A pigsty."

Spencer glanced about the room. It seemed suitable enough to him. Whatever. He was in no mood to haggle. Already the conversation had gone on far longer than he wished.

"Sixty it is." He opened the bottom drawer, took a key from his waistcoat pocket, and lifted the strong box onto the desk. Once he unlocked it, he gathered a handful of pound notes and slid the money across to her. "Is this enough?" He had more in a safe in his room, hidden behind a seaside portrait.

Miss McGrattan descended on the cluster of bills like a falcon swooping in on a field mouse. After a quick count, she tucked the money away in her generous cleavage. His shaft did more than twitch this time.

"Twenty-two pounds all total. The rest will be due when I depart. If any other expenses or inconveniences crop up, we'll negotiate further. Meanwhile, there is plenty of food. I'll see what I can scrounge up. I'll fetch you when it's ready."

Miss McGrattan turned on her heel and marched from the room.

Theodora gave him a questioning woof.

"I know, old girl. I'm not certain what to make of her either."

DURING PHIL'S EXPLORATION of the second floor, she found various rooms in a sorry state of neglect. One room, however, looked quite livable. It must be his lordship's. Most of the furnishings were plain and serviceable, but the cleanliness surprised her. The hag of a housekeeper hadn't kept it spotless. It must be the professor.

In the center of his room was a bed with an ornate wooden frame and headboard decorated with carved scrolls and crests like an aristocrat would own. Gold and brown bedding and rugs matched the draperies. They were open to let in the light. Too bad there weren't any rays of sunshine. Twilight hovered on the horizon, the skies even more ominous than before. Could a storm be brewing? No snow as yet, despite the cold temperatures.

Phil moved to a side alcove where various toiletries were laid out in a neat row. His lordship hadn't seen a razor in several months, but evidence suggested he at least washed; there's a mercy. She lifted the cake of soap to her nose and inhaled. Spicy, she could detect cloves. Shame on her for snooping, but curiosity urged her to continue exploring. In the wardrobe, five white shirts, three pairs of black trousers, and a pair of brown ones hung neatly on hangers.

Pulling open the drawers below, she found socks and smalls folded neatly next to embroidered handkerchiefs. The stitching looked fancy, "SMH" etched in gold thread. She trailed her finger over the initials. Phil couldn't help but smile at the deliberate arrangement of the items in the drawers.

Who in the bloody hell folds their socks?

Closing the wardrobe, she turned in a circle, inspecting the rest of the room. After spying a door on the opposite wall, she opened it.

They are connecting rooms.

Perfect, she would stay here. Or maybe not.

Compared to the professor's room, this one was wholly dilapidated. Numerous plaster cracks were visible on the ceiling and walls, while the faded pink paint showed stains and little maintenance.

Dust motes floated in the air, and the stagnant smell proved the room had been closed up for some time. Considering her limited options, it would have to do. The bed was a good size and comfortable enough for her purposes. Phil pulled off the quilt, and a cloud of dust caused her to cough. She could hang the quilt outdoors tomorrow and freshen it.

There was no decoration, pictures, or personal touches of any kind. There was no wardrobe either, but at least there were a couple of hooks for her garments. Upon opening the small dresser, Phil discovered a set of sheets and a woolen blanket. She lifted them to her nose. Fresh enough to use on the bed.

It was blasted cold; at least she knew how to light a fire. First, air out the room. Once she moved to the window, Phil struggled to slide it upward. It gave way a few inches to allow fresh air to circulate while she prepared the meal.

What to do for supper? It would have to be cold plates, as exhaustion forbade her to attempt anything else.

As for her planned seduction of the hirsute professor, stubborn pride would not allow her to give up and hide in this dusty chamber regardless of his disheveled appearance and physical impediment. Considering the money Hornsby had already paid and the fee she'd collected from his well-meaning friends, she was already ahead in this venture. All she needs to do is cook the meals and stay in her room.

No, Phil would see this through. Her stubbornness reared its head once again.

There's more than one way to skin a cat.

Once she returned to the kitchen, Phil glanced around the room and frowned. Where to begin? Too late to embark on any comprehensive cleaning, but she located a wooden crate where she placed the dirty crockery and pots.

The cupboards held numerous mismatched dishes, with several pieces cracked and chipped in the bargain. Selecting a couple of plates,

Phil wiped them clean. Opening a few of the packages, she smiled at the contents. At least his lordship did not scrimp on the food.

The old biddy housekeeper never bothered with baking, as there were several loaves of fresh bread, rolls, and little frosted cakes—fine cuts of beef and fresh vegetables. Phil could make a stew tomorrow. Fresh grapes. A rare delicacy. The temptation too great to ignore, Phil popped a couple in her mouth. The juicy explosion caused her to moan with pleasure.

Further exploration turned up a larder with a root cellar directly underneath it. Phil climbed down a couple of stairs and surveyed its contents. The area was cold enough. The professor lived too far away for ice delivery, she surmised. Jars of preserves sat on shelves, and a smoked ham hung in the corner. At least this area wasn't excessively filthy. Most of the food could be stored here.

First order of business—supper.

Phil closed the root cellar door, and a puff of dust rose at the impact, causing her to choke. Once in the kitchen, she located a tray and gathered the dishes and food needed for the meal. The professor may be paying her to stay out of sight, but she would ensure she kept up her end of the conversation when they shared the meals.

Anything to break the ice. It wasn't only her stubbornness causing her to forge ahead with what she was hired to do. This was a true challenge.

One that intrigued her.

Chapter 4

SOON AFTER THE MADAM departed, Spencer took the dogs for a long walk, filling their bowls with fresh water upon returning. Thank God Miss McGrattan offered to see to the cooking. Spencer didn't know how to go about it. During his self-imposed solitude, he learned to look after himself to an extent, but cooking remained a puzzle. Besides, the time taken to prepare meals would be better spent on research.

What caused his housekeeper to "do a runner," as Miss McGrattan stated? The older woman at least brought trays of food to him on a steady basis. He paid her well enough for what little she accomplished. Now he would have to go to the bother of trying to hire someone else.

Blasted inconvenience.

Spencer tried to shave every few weeks but became engrossed in his research, and he had allowed the personal grooming slide except for washing. Before returning to his study, he quickly glanced in his bedroom mirror. No wonder Miss McGrattan had compared him to a disheveled fur trapper; he was decidedly unkempt.

A soft knock sounded at the study door. Miss McGrattan poked her head in. "Follow me, Professor, if you want to eat. What about your beasts?" She pointed at his dogs curled up by the fire.

"I will see to them after the meal." Miss McGrattan turned to leave, so he stood. Justinian also began to rise. "Stay, lad." The dog settled by the fire. Spencer followed her to the dining room. He could not remember the last time he stepped foot in it.

"I assume you have a supply of firewood. No time to light the fire, but if you see to your study and bedroom, I'll make sure the fires are lit here, in the kitchen, and the room I'm staying in. Sit, Professor. It's not much of a meal, I'm afraid, fresh bread, cheese, cold ham, tomatoes, and fruit." She sat opposite, hardly glancing his way. "I thought a beef stew would hit the spot for tomorrow's main meal. Does that meet with your approval?"

Once seated, Spencer helped himself to the food. He was not used to someone chattering at him. Spencer's ordered mind found it hard to keep up with the conversation. A dull ache throbbed in his head. It was best that he had a bite to eat and not try to respond.

"I'll take your silence as a yes," she continued, finally meeting his gaze. "Do you have any food preferences? Certain types you don't like? Manner of preparation?"

Was she mocking him?

Spencer searched for ridicule in her expression—there was none. "I don't like tomatoes sliced; I prefer wedges. I also do not like my food touching each other on the plate." He waited for cynical laughter or a cruel slant to her rather luscious mouth. Again, no sign of any scorn. There were more preferences for his food, but he would leave it for now.

"Noted. I found a nice bottle of claret in your larder if you would pour. Bloody hell, the state of your kitchen! Have you ever been down there? I don't recommend it." Miss McGrattan bit into a piece of cheese. "Utter chaos and filth. I shall attempt to tidy the area tomorrow as I cannot cook in such disarray. Do tell, Professor, what research has you cloistered away like a monk in an abbey?"

Spencer filled their glasses. "I am researching the cultural, philosophical, and bureaucratic changes that took place immediately after the fall of the Western Roman Empire." He took a sip, then continued. "And how those changes affected the Eastern Roman Empire, better known as the Byzantine until it fell to the Ottomans in the 15th century."

At last, he found a way to silence her. The madam stared at him as if he had sprouted an extra head.

"I believe your eyes have glazed over, Miss McGrattan." Spencer cut his ham and popped a portion into his mouth.

She gave him a pert smile. "Indeed. I know nothing about which you speak, and I'm not ashamed to admit it. I enjoy reading but stay with the popular novels of the day. History is extremely tedious. I mean, nothing can be done to change it. The people are dead and gone. Why rehash it all?"

Unfortunately, many people thought the same as Miss McGrattan. A burn of exasperation rolled through Spencer. His emotions hadn't been stirred up to this extent in quite some time.

"There is much to be learned from history, Miss McGrattan, or lest we be doomed to repeat it. Indeed, I see marked economic similarities between our present empire and the Byzantine Empire. I do not expect *you* to know, care, or understand." Keeping the irritation out of his voice proved to be arduous.

She dropped her fork on the plate and narrowed her gaze. "What do you mean, sir? I have some education. Do you imply that I'm an ignorant prostitute without a brain in her head? That I know nothing of the world except how to fuck?"

That 16th-century Germanic word caused his insides to dip as a wave of lust clutched him tight, hardening his shaft.

Good God. Did not expect that reaction.

Her angry countenance and the taut line of her lip showed how insulted she was, but the moisture that gathered on her long lashes proved Spencer had also hurt her feelings. Regret filled him, quieting his irritation.

Strange, as he usually didn't respond or acknowledge reactions in others, physical or emotional. His family taught him to recognize and react to certain emotional signs. He should do so here.

In a calm voice, he said, "Please, accept my apology. I do *not* think you are stupid. It's apparent that you are educated. I am sensitive about my research as many have dismissed its importance. It's my whole life. I suppose one could say it consumes me. I've forgotten how to behave in polite company. Forgive me."

Spencer rarely apologized for his behavior. What was the point? He could only be who he was. And because of it, he was often unaware of people's reactions. But he was acutely aware here and regretted his conduct—another surprising development.

Miss McGrattan blinked, then glanced down at her plate. "I guess I'm sensitive about my education—or lack thereof. It wasn't my fault it got cut short—regardless, it's of no import. I didn't mean to insult your life's work."

"Thank you. You accept my apology, then? It's sincerely meant."

And it was, and it defied all his instincts.

"Yes, I accept it."

They continued the meal in silence, the awkwardness hanging between them as a living, breathing thing. His arousal had abated but returned to life whenever he cast clandestine glances at her. Frowning, he turned his attention to his repast. Philomena McGrattan was a lovely creature. Even with her untidy hair and tea-colored eyes weary from her journey, she cut a fine figure.

I'm behaving as a moon-eyed calf, for God's sake.

"I thought after the meal, I would offer my skills to you," she stated.

Spencer choked on a piece of tomato, reaching for the claret to wash it down.

"I meant my skills in men's grooming. I give an excellent shave." Miss McGrattan winked and gave him a sly smile that curled his toes with unexpected pleasure.

Where did that reaction come from?

This could prove to be one of the longest weeks of my life.

Chapter 5

AFTER THE PROFESSOR fed his hulking beasts, he found her in the connecting room, endeavoring to dust.

"Why have you taken this one? There are six others on this floor," he questioned, clearly uncomfortable with her being in close proximity.

Phil followed him through the door into his room and motioned for him to sit. "It contained the least dust, and that isn't saying much. Please remove your waistcoat."

"Why?"

"Remember? I mentioned the shave at dinner?"

He slipped out of his waistcoat and placed it on the back of the chair without replying.

"Professor Hornsby, I will require you to hold a basin before you for the clippings and such. I need to whack at your beard before attempting a shave."

She laid a towel around his neck and, in doing so, caught a whiff of his spicy soap. The masculine scent appealed to her. As she guessed earlier, he at least washed, a joyous discovery.

Despite his haughty manner, his apology at supper astonished her with its depth of earnestness. Though the ancient past bored her to tears, she would happily sit and listen to him talk about any subject, including history. His baritone voice aroused her. Phil imagined him on the stage, the audience in complete rapture over his oration because the professor's voice was liquid molten gold with the smoothness of a fine whiskey. Yes, he could look as wild and unruly as he liked as long as he kept chatting.

When the professor strode into the dining room for the meal, his spine ramrod straight, she was shocked to her core. It had been a struggle to hide her surprised reaction. Not only did Hornsby *not* have a crooked spine, but he was taller than she expected, perhaps two or three inches over six feet. Though slender, his shoulders were broad, and even with the ill-fitting wool trousers and linen shirt, she sensed that there would not be much softness in the flesh. Odd, considering he spent his time sitting at a desk.

Curiosity lay behind her offer to shave him. Phil wanted to see what manner of countenance resided underneath the facial hair and glasses. Speaking of which—she pulled the spectacles from his face and placed them on the nearby table.

"Do you need to wear these all the time?" she asked.

He blinked as if focusing his vision. "No, mainly for close-up work. I wear them out of habit, or else I would misplace them and forget where they were."

How adorable, an absent-minded professor.

His eyes were beautiful. They possessed a shade of blue used in paintings of a summer sky or a turbulent tropical ocean. Leaning in closer, she made a study of them. Flecks of amber were evident in the iris, and a ring of navy blue surrounded the pupil. How stunning they were. Realizing she stared, Phil grabbed the basin and thrust it into his hands.

She should trim his hair first. Phil could not hold a razor steady thanks to her reaction to his gorgeous sapphire-colored eyes. Instead, she tunneled her hands into his mop of hair. The locks were thick and soft, with many shades of brown. It would be a mortal sin to cut it too short. Did she hear a quiet moan come from his lordship? Phil must have imagined it.

Pulling his hair away from his face, she bit her lower lip to keep from smiling. The man's ears stuck out noticeably. She should keep the hair long enough to cover those jug handles. She reached for the scissors and snipped off a chunk of hair.

"What are you doing?" he cried.

Phil tossed the hank of hair into the basin. "Giving you a trim, my lord. You have to admit you need one. Desperately."

"I do not like having my hair cut," he stated plainly.

"Obviously. Shall I continue?"

"I do not know," he whispered.

She could sense his anxiety but didn't understand why. This must be one of his peculiarities, she guessed. Phil would not judge him for it. "What if I manage to do this haircut quickly? Would that help? I can forego the shave as well if you wish."

"It needs to be cut, and I need a shave, so yes, continue as swiftly as you are able."

Phil worked speedily, cutting layers of various lengths and ending at about his jawline. As she trimmed away the excess, his hair fell into attractive waves that framed his face. He looked much neater without the owl glasses and the wild hair, but she had more to do.

"Do sit still, my lord. You are fidgeting far too much. I will start on your mountain man beard next."

"Don't call me that," he murmured.

"What, a mountain man or a lord? You *are* a lord, aren't you?"

"By way of birth. It's not a title I earned or inherited. It's a courtesy because I happen to be the son of a duke. It is patently ridiculous."

"You prefer professor because you earned that, correct? I'll wager to guess you attended only the finest universities, studied hard, and graduated at the top of your class. I admire that. Professor, it is, then." Phil gave his hair a few more snips. Keeping him talking might distract him from his nervousness.

"No, I did not graduate at the top of my class."

She snorted. "I find that hard to believe."

"I found it all quite tedious. My professors never asked important questions of history."

"Important questions?"

"Yes. Such as—why?"

His statement could be construed as arrogant, but no tone of superiority tinged his voice. He spoke matter-of-factly.

Phil trimmed the beard close. Now to shave him. Picking up the razor, she ran her thumb along the blade. *Sharp.*

"I'm curious, Professor. Why go to all the bloody trouble of caring for your shaving implements but not take the extra step of removing your facial hair?" She asked as she soaped up his face.

"I have a certain way of doing things. I prefer my personal belongings arranged in a certain way. I go about my tasks with a definitive approach." There was tension in his voice. "Also, forgoing shaving allows me to use the valuable time for extra research."

The professor was odd, and no mistake.

As she observed before, she wasn't cruel despite all that had happened to her in her past. Phil would never scoff or laugh at his way of doing things. There would be no reaction from her for his myriad, strange habits, like the few he'd mentioned at supper.

"The fact that I'm handling your possessions makes you uncomfortable, correct? And my cutting your hair. Why *did* you agree to the shave?"

Hornsby didn't answer right away.

Phil moved behind him and leaned his head back against her chest. His spicy scent invaded her nostrils again, and the fact he made close contact with her breasts caused another one of those rolls of heat to propel through her with a swift blast.

The blade hovered by his cheek. "Truthfully, I'm not certain," he answered softly. "Usually, I do not like to be—touched."

That explained some of his behavior. "Then I will try not to prolong this."

"I do not mind you—touching me. Please, continue."

She scraped the razor from his chin to his cheek. Phil could not stop exploring his face with the tips of her fingers, for the professor possessed magnificent cheekbones. Once she rinsed the blade, she shaved the right side. Tilting his chin up, she quickly removed the hair on his neck, chin, and under his nose. Once completed, Phil laid a warm, damp towel on his face.

Now for the unveiling. Positioning herself between his spread legs, she gently blotted his face with the towel. Standing near him like this made her heart stutter wildly. With one last wipe, Phil removed the towel.

Oh my.

He was not a classically handsome man as such since his face was a little too long and angular, and his sharp, prominent nose had a bit of a snub on the end. His jawline was adequate, though his chin could be more robust, yet it suited his features. What drew her attention were his lips. They were full and sensual with a perfect cupid's bow.

Such a perfect mouth, and on a man, no less.

Hornsby possessed one of the most striking, unusual, and enthralling faces she had ever beheld. Her breath seized while her heart thumped against her ribcage. No denying the fact, she was attracted to this man. He *was* handsome, to her at least. What to say?

I did not expect this reaction at all.

"Are you quite well, Miss McGrattan? You seem to be in a state of shock."

The melodious voice completed the fascinating portrait. Phil could not stop herself from cupping his face, her thumbs stroking those perfectly sculpted cheekbones. Hornsby gazed up at her. His brows furrowed in what she imagined could be confusion.

"You, my dear Professor—captive me."

HER GENTLY SPOKEN WORDS arrowed straight to his soul. She could not mean it. Glaring at his reflection in the mirror over the years showed clear proof that he was not as attractive as his older brothers. Spencer studied her, trying to find any hint of malicious mockery, but none were visible. Miss McGrattan—Philomena—leaned closer.

"Are you going to kiss me?" he asked, the words escaping before he could stop them.

"Would you object if I did? Your lips *are* eminently kissable."

A hot flush spread across his cheeks and neck, covering his whole body.

Blast my inexperience.

Spencer tore his gaze from hers and closed his eyes, embarrassed at his reaction. If she dared to glance downward, she would observe one of the most painful erections ever since he was capable of having them.

All this from a woman touching and shaving him, stroking his cheeks, and telling him that he captivated her. Surprisingly, since Spencer didn't like being touched all that much, and having his hair cut caused sensory anxiety that, to this day, he could not understand. Yet, with Miss McGrattan, the stress was not nearly as intense. Almost non-existent.

What an easy seduction he'd be for this knowledgeable temptress, and that thought rankled to his core. As vulnerable as an untried boy, which he supposed he was in reality.

It's not that he'd never experienced desire. There were one or two occasions, though nothing came of it. Spencer believed making love should not be something casual to scratch a particular carnal itch but should be revered and savored.

On the other hand, if it never happened at all, he wouldn't care. What passion he possessed was funneled into his research, and any emotions were reserved for his dogs and his family.

Spencer was convinced there was no desire or feelings left over for anyone else. Who needs complicated emotions to muck things up and disturb his well-ordered life?

By that standard, how could Philomena do this for a living? And why was he thinking of her by her first name? It made everything she said—and what he read in her expression—counterfeit.

He opened his eyes, grasped her arms, and pushed her away. "I do not want to be kissed."

Philomena gave him a quirky smile. "Quite right. Too soon. It's something that has to be worked up to with slow anticipation. The expectancy of it can be thrilling. First, a touch—a brush of fingers against bare skin."

Philomena opened the buttons on his shirt, exposing his upper chest. She trailed the tips of two fingers across his collarbone, causing him to shudder with desire.

"A feather-like touch, enough to ignite the sparks of skin against skin," she continued. "To know what bliss can be found when two naked bodies come in contact. The warmth, the scent, the act of becoming one."

God in heaven, she seduced him with huskily spoken words and a barely-there touch. His insides turned to liquid, his bones to jelly. Spencer was putty in her hands, and she no doubt knew it. However, she was not smug about the knowledge, a fire burned in her light brown eyes. Philomena was as affected as he.

Astounding.

Exploring, she stroked the hollow of his throat with the tip of her finger. Try as he might, Spencer could not resist a moan of desire.

"If you are at all uncomfortable with me touching you? Say the word, and I will stop."

"Don't—stop."

Philomena leaned in close, her warm, sultry breath igniting his skin. "Don't think I'm pulling this out of my prossie bag of tricks. I will tell you a secret. By my choice, I've not been with a man for a few years. Sex has always been a chore for me. You're the first man to make me anticipate it." She caressed his cheek, then stepped away, the spell broken. "I'm exhausted. It's been a long day. Goodnight, Professor."

With his coat off, his arousal would not be hard to miss. His emotions were running the gambit, and his insides were in knots. Regardless, Spencer stood and did something he'd never done before. Clasping her hand, he brought it to his lips and let it hover there momentarily, a mere inch from contact. He had observed his older brothers do this with women enough. His gaze swept upward and captured hers. Her eyes were bright, her breathing shallow.

Yes, the anticipation. It pounded between them with a potent force.

Spencer kissed her hand while he stroked the pulse point at her wrist with his thumb. The beat throbbed and raced under his touch. Reluctantly, he released her.

"Goodnight and pleasant dreams...Philomena."

After giving him a slight, but unsteady curtsy, Philomena retreated.

Exhaling shakily, Spencer stared at the closed door. His first reaction to this preposterous scenario was to reject her reason for being here and ensure that she stayed in her room, out of his sight and mind, until her departure.

After observing her reaction to his touch?

Being a man of research, the best course is to let this play out to whatever conclusion.

Miss McGrattan was not the only one utterly captivated.

Chapter 6

DAYLIGHT FILTERED THROUGH the green curtains, though Phil didn't know the time. She yawned and stretched. Slumber did not come easily last night, not at first. If it wasn't for the utter exhaustion, she would have stayed and explored the attraction between her and the professor. When he kissed her hand and stroked the skin at her wrist, her body surged with desire. For a man of little to no experience, he certainly learned quickly.

No need to sugarcoat it.

She was a prostitute—and had been since the age of fifteen. In all her varied encounters, she'd never experienced much of anything. To see the job through, Phil often used unguents and creams. Nevertheless, touching Spencer Hornsby the previous night caused a physical response. A shocking discovery indeed.

Along with her lubrications, Phil also packed quite a few sheaths. Too many women in her acquaintance took ill with infections and diseases. Be damned if that would be her fate.

Enough thoughts of sex and arousal.

Phil swung her legs around the side of the bed and sat upright. Despite how society viewed her occupation, she was proud that she built her business up from renting a few rooms to owning the house outright. Could the Starling Club function in her absence? She could not contact her employees to let them know she would be gone for more than two days. Good thing she'd hired competent people. Darius would see to it. They would soldier on. She hoped.

With a sigh, Phil strode to the window and threw open the draperies. A puff of dust hung in the air, and she waved it away. No sunlight. The clouds were grayer and more ominous than yesterday. No doubt about it, a snowstorm loomed on the horizon.

What if she remained stuck in this forsaken place for over a week? What if the old man could not traverse the snow-laden roads with his rickety grocery cart? Well, there was enough food to last them at least a few weeks should it come to that. The air outside was utterly still. There wasn't another living soul for miles. How eerie.

Enough shillyshallying. There is much to do.

Phil desperately needed a bath to wash off the travel grime and the dust from this place. She might as well tidy the kitchen before partaking of a bath. Seeing there was no indoor water closet, she assumed there wouldn't be any running water connected to a tub. How primitive. Already she bemoaned the loss of her modern bathroom at her club.

Phil dressed in her green gown, styled her hair in a serviceable knot and went downstairs. The door was closed to the study, indicating the professor no doubt toiled away inside. After using the outdoor privy located through the kitchen entrance, she rolled up her sleeves and prepared breakfast.

Forty minutes later, Phil stood outside the study. No use knocking since he hadn't responded yesterday. She opened the door and froze in place. Spencer Hornsby knelt before the roaring fireplace and lifted a small quilt from the mantel. He laid the blanket on one of the dogs. The beast whimpered and gave the professor such a look of love and devotion that a ball of emotion caught in Phil's throat. With gentle strokes, he rubbed the warmed cloth over the animal.

"There, my dear old girl. Would I hazard to guess that feels good? Your poor aching muscles." He crooned to the dog, soothing the canine as he spoke. The words were filled with gentle concern. "We've been together a good long time, Theodora. Eleven years. I would like eleven more if we can manage it." Theodora affectionately licked the professor's hand. The other dog lay next to Theodora. "That's the good boy, Justinian. Keep your mum warm. Good lad."

Phil backed away, wiping her eyes. Why on earth had she teared up? Perhaps, for once in her life, she wanted someone to wrap her in a warm blanket and whisper words of comfort. Maybe she wished for Spencer Hornsby to soothe and reassure her.

Envious of a dog, bloody hell, what next?

Taking a deep breath, she regained control of her rampant sentimentality and re-entered the room.

"BREAKFAST IN THE DINING room, Professor." Her voice was cold and officious, and Spencer raised an eyebrow at her tone. Before he could respond, she turned on her heel and departed.

Philomena's demeanor perplexed him. He glanced at Justinian. They exchanged puzzled looks, and he said, "No lad, I don't understand women either."

Spencer made his way to the dining room. The fire was lit, and warmth filled the area. On the table were fried eggs, a rasher of bacon, thick slices of fresh bread, and a pot of tea. He sat opposite.

"This is a rare treat. I usually do not eat breakfast." He preferred his eggs poached but would not make extra demands.

"Well, you're too thin, if you don't mind me saying. I'm a firm believer in a hearty breakfast. Sets you up for the day ahead."

Nodding, he buttered a piece of bread. "I've lost weight since I arrived here. Sometimes I become engrossed in my work and forget to eat."

"Your animals—"

"They are my friends as well as my companions," he interjected.

"Yes, I can see that. Where did you get them?"

"I acquired Theodora first. When I turned nineteen, I decided I wanted a dog. Father initially objected as I would be away at university, 'Who would look after the beast?' However, my dear mother talked him around. A few years after I graduated, I had a mind to breed her. She accompanied me on a trip to northern England to a man who bred Irish Wolfhounds. Soon after, she was with the pup." He hesitated. Conversation did not come easy for him; he hadn't spoken this much in ages.

Yet, he was at ease in Philomena's presence. Astounding since most conversations with others filled him with anxiety. Not here. Nibbling on a piece of bacon, he swallowed, then continued. "There were difficulties with the birth. Thank God a doctor from the Veterinary College practiced nearby. He saved her life and that of her son. The other pup, a female, did not survive. Theodora had to be spayed; no more puppies for her. They've both been with me ever since."

"They mean a lot to you." She smiled at him, her eyes softening. Her warm expression caused his heart to skip a beat.

"Yes, they do."

"Ever thought of breeding Justinian?"

"Yes. I have. I would want one of the puppies. I will look into the matter when I return home." Whenever that would be, he had no immediate plans to leave Wales.

"Interesting names. Where did you get them?" Philomena asked as she bit into her bread.

He briefly returned her smile as this was one of his favorite subjects. "Theodora was an empress in the Byzantine Empire from 527 to 548 AD. She had a rather interesting past. Before being an empress, she acted on stage, served in a brothel, and later was the mistress of a Syrian official. Her beauty was admired, as well as her humor and charm. Tired of her lascivious life, Theodora returned to Constantinople, where she became a wool spinner near the palace. She caught the eye of

Justinian, heir to the throne. Such a low association could not be borne. His family, particularly his mother, objected to the connection."

He paused. After all, he was not standing behind a lectern. He must be boring her silly.

"Here endeth the lecture," he murmured.

But she was not disinterested at all. Instead, Philomena sat forward, her chin resting on her hand as she listened with rapt attention to his every word.

"She was an actress—and a prostitute," she whispered. "Please continue. What happened next?"

"Justinian would not settle for any other woman. An ancient Roman law prohibited government officials from marrying an actress, so he bided his time. When his mother passed, the current emperor—his uncle—repealed the law, and the couple married."

Philomena clapped her hands with delight. "How romantic!"

Spencer could not help but be pleased with her enthusiasm. "Theodora worked at his side, a co-ruler essentially. They brought about many modern reforms together, but they also clashed over religious issues. Regardless of their differences, he loved her to the end."

"Will you tell me more, perhaps tonight after supper?" Philomena sipped her tea, watching him over the rim.

The fact that she showed genuine interest in his research gratified him more than it should. "I would be honored to do so."

"Excellent! You know, I believe it will snow. Have you seen the skies? Most ominous looking, to be sure."

Spencer could not tear his gaze from her. Her chatter faded into mist. He allowed the unfamiliar emotions to spin through him, which gave him more peace than he'd ever known. A woman was interested in what he had to say.

Pray, let it not be a lie.

His heart could not take such a falsehood. He'd been cruelly ridiculed   for   years   for   his   dogged   pursuit   of   historical investigation—and for the foibles of his strange personality. His own family didn't understand him or his passion for intense study. He understood enough to realize that the research served as an escape from the realities of the world. It allowed him to hide from dealing with people and with issues of everyday life. It gave him a sense of calm contentment that he did not have in his early years.

Spencer did not possess that particular talent for conversing with others. And yet he felt comfortable talking with Philomena—quite the revelation. There was something about her that soothed him—made him *feel*. What emotions exactly was hard to ascertain.

"I would like to have a bath, Professor. How can that be achieved?" Philomena asked, pulling him from his intense thoughts.

The thought of her lounging naked in his tub caused his wayward emotions to spark. "I will bring the tub to the kitchen and assist you with filling it. It is far easier than bringing buckets of water upstairs. I use it down here. It is more efficient."

"Yes, that makes sense. Let us do that. I will tidy the kitchen first and let you know when I am ready for the bath. Is that all right?"

"Yes, that is sufficient."

Exhaling, he ran his last bit of bread through the egg yolk on his plate, wiped his mouth on the napkin, stood, and headed toward the door. Best that he returned to his research and kept his mind focused elsewhere. And not on a certain golden red-haired beauty.

"Professor Hornsby. Happy birthday."

That's right. My thirtieth birthday.

Turning to face her, he gave a slight bow. "Many thanks, Miss McGrattan."

He sauntered into the hall, his step a little more jaunty than usual.

A happy birthday indeed.

Chapter 7

PHIL DIDN'T USUALLY clean a room while wearing nothing but her shift; however, she didn't have much choice. With only two gowns in her current possession, soiling one with kitchen grease was undesirable. A thorough clean-up would take days, but Phil wanted the place organized, especially if she were to labor here preparing meals.

After removing the rubbish from the floor, she washed the dishes, at least the ones that were salvageable. The professor had stated he didn't require any lunch as he was still too full from breakfast. She helped herself to a plate of bread and cheese, then immediately began preparing the beef stew.

Phil had forgotten how much she enjoyed cooking. There wasn't much use for it since she employed a woman at the Starling Club to see to the meals. Years ago, she gave up all hope of ever having her own home. For a week, she could make believe she was the lady of the house. Perhaps not "lady" in the strictest societal sense, but at least she could make this kitchen her temporary domain. Why not indulge in the fantasy? Whistling, she scrubbed the counter with a little more vigor.

A gruff woof startled her from her chore. Phil whirled around. One of the dogs stood in the middle of the kitchen with its head cocked.

"Ah. I believe you're Justinian. I noticed the gray in your fur has a deeper shade than your mother's. Other than that, it's hard to tell you apart unless I lift your tail. Well, I suppose, being younger, you stand a little taller, don't you, lad?"

Justinian answered with a woof and a nod of his head. Phil couldn't help but laugh. It was as if the beast understood her. Holding out her hand, she allowed the dog to sniff it.

"I'm not the enemy. I am happy to make your acquaintance." She spoke in a calm tone. The canine rubbed his head against her in a gesture of acceptance. "Well. Looking for affection. I wonder if your master is looking for the same. What is it he said? 'Gentle when stroked.' Let's see if that applies to you, my handsome boy."

The animal was enormous, a canine giant whose fur was wiry but supple to the touch. Because he was so big, she didn't have to crouch down to pet him. "Do you like cheese, I wonder?" She snatched a piece from her lunch plate and held it out for him. With a quick twitch of his nose, Justinian nibbled it gently from her hand.

A cough from the direction of the entrance caused her to jump. There stood the professor, his face bright and his beautiful blue eyes glittering with emotion. He gripped the handle of the wooden tub. How much had he heard of her silly conversation with the wolfhound?

IN HER SEMI-TRANSPARENT shift, Philomena stood as a vision, every luscious curve apparent. Her breasts were stunning, and the nipples were clearly visible through the sheer material, the peaks pushing against the cloth. He ached to touch her, stroke her breasts, and feel those hard nubs between his fingers.

He was never aroused like this before, and the strange euphoria was hard to fathom. He had read of men through history losing their heads—sometimes literally—over a woman but never understood why. Now he had a suspicion as to the cause.

Spencer heard every word she spoke to Justinian. At this moment, he envied the dog. He yearned for Philomena to touch him as gently as she touched his dog. His gaze took in the sensual curve of her hip. He admired the sight, approving of the goddess before him.

"I-I-I-" Good God, he stuttered like a green lad. He swallowed hard.

Try again, you fool.

"I brought the tub. I can help you fill it if you like. You said you would let me know, but I surmised you might wish it now." The words tumbled out of him in a rush, annoying him further.

Philomena placed a hand on her hip while the other continued to pet Justinian. "Thank you for your offer of assistance. I would like the bath right now." She gave him a brief, sweet smile, enough to cause his insides to dip again. "I couldn't very well clean with one of my gowns on. I only have the two with me. I suppose I could have attempted it naked."

A sensual vision of her nude on her hands and knees scrubbing the floor with a slow, sensual motion while her breasts swayed with each pull and drag of the cloth caused a forceful stab of lust to shoot through him. He dropped the tub, his mouth going dry.

Words failed him.

Spencer revealed too much, and it irked him. Did she tease him because he stood before her, gawking as a simpleton might? Or was she even teasing? He had no way of knowing for sure. He had no control and cursed at himself for his outward reaction.

Philomena stepped away from the dog and faced him. "Do you like what you see?"

The tone of her voice did not mock nor tease; in fact, she sounded deadly serious.

"I do indeed." Spencer was not going to lie. Not about this. "You are a lovely specimen."

"Ever the professor."

She trailed her hand down his chest, then lingered at the waistband of his trousers. The stroke of her fingers across his stomach caused his muscles to tighten.

"You're solidly built." Her expression held what he supposed could be desire.

Hard to distinguish, as no woman ever gazed at him with such concentration or heat. Philomena's fingers brushed by his semi-erect shaft, causing it to harden further. She cupped him between his legs, and a groan of yearning escaped him.

"My, how intoxicating," she murmured huskily.

A squeeze of his cock was all it took.

Spencer groaned and shuddered as he spent in his trousers. A wave of mortification covered him as he turned from her, embarrassed to the depths of his marrow. He should leave, but his shaky legs wouldn't move. His breathing became uneven. Finally, his limbs snapped into action, and he sprinted for the door.

"Wait, Spencer. Please don't go." Her words were softly spoken. Philomena came up behind him and embraced him tight, her full breasts pressed against his back. "Don't be ashamed," she murmured. "Completely expected and understandable. I shouldn't have touched you so intimately, but I couldn't help myself. The way you looked at me. It moved and aroused me in ways I'm not used to feeling. I ..." Her voice caught. Philomena exhaled. "You will learn better control as you gain knowledge. It's nothing to be humiliated about. You had a natural reaction, and I'm extremely flattered."

She nuzzled his back, her warmth comforting. Her stark honesty humbled him. One of her hands lay flat on his chest.

Spencer placed his hand on top of hers. "My inexperience is quite obvious," he answered, trying for levity but failing as his voice shook with emotion.

"I can assist you with that, Spencer. We have the week before us."
She sighed. "I want you, and not in a business sense. It's an unknown
yearning for me. Let us take this journey together."

Her words were genuine, but he was not the best judge when it
came to assessing another person's emotions and statements. The offer
sorely tempted him. Something nagged and twisted his insides,
however. He was a lanky, awkward creature; why would such a
splendid-looking woman want to be bothered with him in any way?

Would she return to London and share her adventure with others,
laughing at his discomfited bearing? Old insecurities died hard; they
clung stubbornly to one's soul. Perhaps this would be one way to banish
them. As he thought before, researching this could prove helpful. Or
perhaps it provided a ready excuse to move ahead with the seduction.

What to do?

"I must go. I need to...." He puffed out a shaky breath. Why fight
this? "Very well, Miss McGrattan. If you have things to teach me, I am
not averse to learning."

She gave him a brief hug and stepped away. He mourned the loss of
her comforting affection. "Please, call me Phil. May I call you Spence?
Your friends referred to you as such."

Only his family and friends called him Spence. He preferred
Spencer but never bothered to inform anyone about it. What would be
the harm? It evoked a certain intimacy he was not sure he wished for or
was able to comprehend. But gazing into her lovely eyes, he could not
deny her.

"Yes, if you wish."

Spencer hurried from the room without looking back. It was best
to take his leave before he changed his mind. As soon as he was out
of her sight, he ran up the stairs, taking them two at a time. Justinian
followed on his heels.

On some level, Spencer must want this—encounter—to proceed, for he made no move to quell it. He hoped he was not making a mistake.

Chapter 8

CONCENTRATING ON HIS research the rest of the afternoon proved next to impossible. Spencer's mind shifted back and forth between feeling mortified at his loss of control or imagining Phil lounging naked in the tub, the soap traversing every curve of her magnificent body.

Phil was correct about the impending nasty weather as the atmosphere was gloomy, indeed. He gazed out the window. A few snowflakes tumbled from the gray sky.

He planned to remain at this isolated place until early spring, then reveal his findings to the British Museum. If all went well, Spencer would ultimately present his research to the history department of Oxford University, hoping to convince them to introduce the subject matter to the curriculum with him teaching the class. He could manage to speak before a room of students if he concentrated on the subject and did not look out into the sea of humanity sitting before him. At least, he hoped that would be the case.

While school held many horrors for him, he found immense satisfaction in the education overall. Although he possessed an interest in the study of Greek and Latin, he believed Oxford relied too much on it.

Spencer used to disparage his classmates—and his two older brothers, for that matter—for the time they wasted chasing after women with the sole purpose of sex. He sniffed in disdain at them all, for he possessed a higher calling: the pursuit of knowledge and understanding. It was far loftier than the hunt for a bed partner.

"Just wait, Spence. One day luscious female curves will strike you; mark my words!"

His oldest brother, Harrison, and heir to the dukedom, had declared the inane statement. Did Harry speak the truth? Apparently, if all a woman had to do was brush her fingers across his prick, turning him into a mass of pathetic ingenuousness.

As soon as he left Phil in the kitchen, he ran to his room, stripped down, then washed thoroughly. His small clothes and trousers were soaking in the basin while he changed into fresh attire. Last night Phil commented on the fact that he did not like someone handling his possessions. How astute of her. His own father called him peculiar, and that had been said with affection.

He thought he'd be uncomfortable having a strange woman in the house. He didn't count the housekeeper as he barely saw her from one day to the next. Spencer looked after himself and his room and even washed his clothes because he did not want anyone handling them. Yes, peculiar. But he learned to live with the man he was and accept him.

Something else occupied his thoughts all afternoon.

The shocking fact is that he agreed to allow Phil to seduce him. He agreed to *sex*. Perhaps he was as his older brother delicately described. Allowing her to touch him more intimately than she already had would require trust on his part and placing his trepidations aside.

Another thing that astounded him: was Phil claiming she'd not been with a man for a few years. He had no idea what a prostitute did or did not do with her customers. A picture filled his mind of Phil on a bed with her legs spread, a bored look on her face while a man grunted on top of her. He shook the disturbing vision from his mind. Would she have the same expression while he thrust into her?

Yes, old insecurities die hard, indeed.

A steady knock at the door, and Phil poked her head in. "Dinner is served, Spence."

She spoke warmly, and hearing his name on her lush lips caused his insides to tumble. Justinian lifted his head and gave her a friendly and welcoming woof. She made friends with his pet. Astonishing.

"My handsome lad."

"Are you talking to Justinian or me? I assume you mean the dog." What possessed him to say that?

Phil's gaze swept upward and locked with his. "The both of you, of course."

"Now I know you are fibbing."

"I have not spoken any falsehoods to you ever, Spence. I never will." Her tone was firm and determined. In response, his heart banged in his chest with a fierce beat.

Spencer followed her to the dining room, and on the table sat a tureen of stew brimming with cuts of beef and assorted vegetables like potatoes and carrots, all swimming in a thick gravy. There were also slices of bread and a platter of fruit and cheeses.

Philomena filled his bowl and passed it to him. Spencer inhaled. It smelled delicious. He could make out the odors of onion, celery, and thyme.

"Did you have a productive afternoon?" Philomena asked as he generously buttered the fresh bread.

"No."

"Oh? I am sorry to hear it. I interrupted your work, didn't I, with all that noise in the kitchen and then seeing to my bath. I am sorry for that. I will endeavor not to disturb you in the future. I imagine you need complete silence for your research."

She did interrupt his work, but not as she claimed. Spencer could hardly tell her that she filled his thoughts, blocking out everything else.

"I will adjust. I often do." Spencer took a spoonful of the stew. It was far better than anything Mrs. Brickell had managed. He should offer a compliment. "This is very tasty."

"I am glad you like it. I always enjoyed eating stew, whether it be beef, mutton, or chicken. It is such a hearty meal, isn't it? It warms the insides and gives a feeling of comfort. Everything is all in one bowl. So efficient." Philomena paused. "Do I annoy you with all this small talk?"

Spencer looked up. "Not anymore."

Philomena laughed heartily. Had he said something funny? It was hard to know.

They continued eating, and Spencer even had a second helping. Phil cleared away the dishes and placed a covered platter in front of him.

"What is this?" he asked.

Phil lifted the cover. In the center of the plate was a large candle surrounded by petite frosted cakes. She struck a match and lit the wick.

"Happy birthday, Spence! Make a wish. I would've baked you a cake, but I haven't attempted baking in so long that I would have made a hash of it. With the cleaning, preparing the stew, my bath, well—there was no bloody time." Phil waved her arm toward the table. "The cakes were included in your food order. Not sure what they are."

Her gesture genuinely moved him. Without thinking, Spencer clasped her hand and squeezed it, then lifted it to his lips to kiss it. Touching her was a never-ending delight. God above, he never touched anyone except when he could not avoid it. Leaning forward, he blew and snuffed out the candle. Why not make a wish?

I want the warmth and kindness that she shows toward me to be genuine. Pray, let it be so.

Phil clapped with enthusiasm.

"I believe Mrs. Brickell had a sweet tooth. I've never seen these before." He picked one up and bit into it. Pound cake with raspberry jam in the center is covered with a rich butter frosting, which is quite sinful. Spencer held it out to her. Would she feed from his hand? An intimate act, to be certain, and not like him at all.

Phil leaned in and nibbled, her tongue darting outward to lick his finger. The thrilling sensation almost caused him to lose his hold on the cake.

"Delicious. I found a bottle of German white wine in the root cellar. Shall we open it in celebration of your birthday?" She passed him the bottle and the corkscrew. "We can lounge before the fire as Justinian and Theodora do."

He nodded as he glanced at the fireplace. Spencer hadn't noticed it when he first entered the room. A few cushions and a blanket were arranged before the hearth.

They settled in among the pillows. Spencer poured the wine and passed her a glass.

Phil raised it. "Happy Birthday."

He clinked his goblet against hers and took a sip. As they drank and ate the cakes silently, Spencer couldn't tear his eyes from her and found the quiet contemplation between them reassuring.

Occasionally, Phil would meet his gaze while nibbling on the cake. The logs snapped and crackled; the fire cast a soothing golden glow making her red hair all the more vibrant. He caught a whiff of lavender.

It must be her soap. Very alluring.

"I cannot remember when I've enjoyed such a pleasant birthday. Thank you, Phil." There. He managed another compliment. And it was sincerely meant.

"Do you often celebrate special occasions by yourself?" she asked.

"As of late, yes, I have. Not that I celebrate any occasions all that often. I am not one for parties. Crowds of people overwhelm me. I find it hard to breathe. My family tries to understand."

Again, he revealed far more than intended. Change the subject or disclose his private thoughts? Or keep quiet altogether? He decided to soldier on.

"I've often wondered if I was adopted, a foundling from an orphanage, or as my family often teased, found abandoned on a pile of cordwood. And although a joke, it genuinely terrified me as I was born in early winter and often wondered what would have become of me if my parents hadn't come along."

Phil chuckled, and he was pleased he made a semblance of a joke. "I am nothing like my family," he continued. "Both my parents and two brothers are gregarious and social. The house is usually filled with guests. My brothers are quite the handsome rakes and eagerly sought in society. Alas, I do not fit in." Spencer sipped his wine, wondering if he *had* revealed too much.

Truthfully, he was better off alone.

Too many painful memories of awkward situations kept him well secluded. He preferred it—but not tonight.

"Phil. Can you tell me about your past? How did you—well, how—?"

"Did I become a harlot? Is that what you want to bloody well know?" she snapped irritably.

"It's none of my business. Forgive my crass question."

Phil shrugged, then sighed. "I have a bit of a temper; the red shade of my hair is no lie. Sorry."

"If you would rather not talk about it, I understand," he offered.

"No. You revealed something of yourself. I will do the same. There is a seamy underbelly to society that most decent people cannot comprehend. My parents died, and, at age thirteen, I went to live with my aunt and uncle. They were not bad as guardians go. A little strict and pious, perhaps, but I was not ill-treated. One late afternoon when I was around fifteen years of age, my aunt and I were about to catch a train to visit her sister in Brighton."

Phil paused and rubbed her hands nervously as if uncomfortable revealing her past. Taking a deep breath, she exhaled and continued. "While on the platform, my aunt realized she'd neglected to buy the right class of ticket. We were about to head to the ticket window when a well-dressed, older lady stepped forward and offered to watch over me while my aunt attended to her task. My aunt agreed. I was then led behind a pillar where a foul-smelling cloth covered my face. When next I awoke, I found myself in a brothel in Belfast."

Horrified and shocked, Spencer's mouth dropped open. "My God."

"Thankfully, the madam in charge of the place was not an absolute reprobate. For the next several months, I trained and was brought into the life slowly. What could I do, run? I was in a strange country with no money. The best way to make coin?"

Phil let the statement dangle. She crossed her arms in defiance as if daring him to react. He didn't.

"I became a prostitute. I made a vow. Never would I be one of those poor unfortunates begging for a quick shilling tup in a smelly alley. I would make damn sure I had a roof over my head and food in my belly. By the time I turned eighteen, I had saved enough money to head home. To say my aunt and uncle were not best pleased to see me is an understatement."

She frowned, then took a great gulp of wine. Spencer could not believe this. Her story had the makings of a dark tale written by Dickens. Did such things occur? Innocents taken into slavery. Yet, his historical research showed that this occurred throughout history and no doubt would in the decades to come. It boggled his mind. His heart swelled with sympathy and compassion. Again, emotions he was not used to feeling or showing.

He reached for her hand and held it tight. "You told them what happened. You could hardly be blamed."

Her lower lip quivered. The first sign of vulnerability from her, and it warmed his heart that she showed it to him.

"To them, I had sinned beyond all redemption. I was a fallen woman, a jezebel. They tossed me out and claimed they never wanted to see me again. Yes, it hurt. But I walked away and immediately found one of the best brothels in West London. I had no other skills. No other recourse. No one else to turn to. I took responsibility for my own life and haven't looked back."

A tear trailed down her flushed cheek. Spencer didn't give comfort to people. It meant touching and offering "there, there" platitudes he often did not feel. The rush of emotions that flooded him at this moment—stunned him. He embraced her, stroking her luxuriant golden-red hair hanging loose about her shoulders. Tucking her head under his chin, he decided for once to be compassionate.

She cried quietly into his shirt.

And he let her.

Chapter 9

AT FIRST, SPENCE'S embrace revealed the stiff awkwardness of a man not used to offering comfort. Then he touched her hair and softened all around her, encasing her in his tender embrace.

Phil burrowed into his linen shirt, inhaling the wonderful scent he emanated: spice and a musky, masculine aroma that soothed her. The tears would not stop. They trailed down her cheeks, no doubt drenching his fine shirt. Phil did not sob hysterically but cried a cleansing release of everything she held in for such a long time.

In all these years, she never spoke of her past to anyone.

Why Spencer Hornsby?

A man she had known barely two days. Perhaps after witnessing his vulnerability when he had spent in his trousers ad him making other revelations, she allowed the thorns around her heart not to be quite as tangled and painful. His susceptibility gave voice to her own.

Phil moved closer. How she wanted him. An overwhelming need to push him on his back, straddle and ride him until they both cried from blessed sensual relief, clouded her sensibilities. No man stirred such passion in her before.

Take things slowly.

She would have to start things gradually, building up to what she now understood would be a soul-shattering experience between them. Things between them moved far too swiftly—but she had no power to stop this, whatever "this" was.

Stroking his chest, she marveled at the solidity of him. More muscle there than she would have guessed. Would he welcome a kiss? He refused one yesterday. With a slow ascent, Phil curled her hand around his neck and pulled him toward her parted lips. His blue-gem eyes glittered with emotions such as surprise, desire, and trepidation. With the barest of contact, her mouth brushed against his perfect one. The reaction could only be described as scorching.

Spence froze as if not sure what to do. Phil nibbled on his full lower lip, savoring the supple feel of it.

"Cup my face with your hands and stare into my eyes. Make me believe this kiss is all-encompassing and needed for your very existence," she instructed.

"It is," he answered, his tone husky.

Oh, my.

That caused a few more tears to escape. Spence did as she directed. His hands radiated warmth and strength. Sparks moved through her as he stroked her cheeks and jaw with the pads of his thumbs.

"Kiss me, Spence," she pleaded.

Capturing her lips with his, he tilted his head to the side and delved deeper. He did so by degrees, and when Phil darted her tongue out to touch his, he started, then moaned and followed her lead.

It went on for some time as they both explored, their tongues dancing together with perfect symmetry. The longer the kiss lasted, the bolder Spence became. Phil sensed his confidence grow with each nibble and lick of his glorious lips. He all but devoured her, and she gave it back and more.

Slowly he pulled back, looking at her with awe. "Is it always like this?"

"I don't kiss as a rule, but no. I've never...ever. No." She caressed his cheek, her thumb stroking the perfect carve of the bone. "Haven't you kissed anyone before?"

"Once, at fifteen. I made quite the specimen with my lanky legs and arms. I also hadn't grown into my nose yet, though I wonder if I ever have. I kissed an earl's daughter by the hedgerow. A sloppy disaster, as I acted like an overeager puppy. She laughed and ridiculed me in front of the others. It was a social gathering, you see. I suppose that could be pinpointed as the moment I began to abhor parties, crowds, and young misses, more than I ever had before. I vowed to avoid them at all costs."

His poignantly spoken words touched her heart. Phil could easily picture what he described. The awkward young man flushed with embarrassment while everyone pointed and laughed. Children could be so bloody cruel.

Should they continue kissing? Perhaps not. Already it overwhelmed her senses. More wine. A moment to breathe and collect her thoughts. Slow and deliberate would win the game. Only this was neither a game nor an assignment any longer.

When she first heard his glorious cello-sounding voice—she was lost. Captivated by his innocence and inexperience, stunned at her reaction to his tall, angular frame and enthralling face, how astonishing to find a generous and passionate heart lurking within this man of intellect and academia.

Remaining vigilant was necessary, or she would be carried away on a wave of wayward emotions. It could not even be considered. An erudite son of a duke would not be the fit companion for a prossie. Sadness dampened her mood as she reached for the wine and poured them more. She passed him the glass.

Giving him a tremulous smile, she said, "Then we shall do all we can to banish such painful memories."

Phil meant every word.

SPENCER EXPERIENCED all conceivable emotions throughout his thirty years. He was a sensitive boy, and other children innately sensed it. They honed in on it as a weakness, which made him an easy target for ridicule. Not as good-looking as his older brothers, Harrison and Tremain, young ladies showed no interest in him. At least his brothers did not treat him cruelly as the other children. His brothers were his protectors as well as his friends. They still were.

Through the spitefulness of others, Spencer learned to remove himself from feeling much of anything. He set up a room in his mind to escape when emotions overwhelmed him. At this moment, sipping wine with Phil, the walls of that private room tumbled down, and feelings long hidden away reemerged into his consciousness with all the power of a tidal wave.

Caution would be needed.

He was intelligent enough to comprehend that expecting more from this brief encounter would not be wise. From what Phil told him, she'd been hurt in her past. How could she not be? Taken from her guardians and her innocence ripped away, she adjusted to her new life state in order to survive.

Brave, courageous woman.

Spencer admired her. Hell, he *liked* her. He didn't give a damn that she was a prostitute. Instead, he thought her the most fascinating woman he'd ever met. There weren't many ladies in his acquaintance, but he met enough through the years to make a competent judgment.

Phil asked him more about Theodora and Justinian —the historical figures, not the dogs. For the next hour, he narrated the facts as a story. She gave him her rapt attention; her eyes shined with curiosity. They drained the wine bottle and ate the small cakes. His stomach roiled at the sugary sweetness.

"Spence, I must confess. Your voice does things to me. From the first time I heard it. I could listen to you speak on any subject, not to say what you've been discussing isn't interesting. You should be on stage. I adore your voice."

The praise pleased him. He never gave his tone of voice much thought before, as he rarely spoke to anyone beyond a few sentences.

"I am contemplating teaching as an option if Oxford University will accept my research when it is completed."

"You claim that you don't like crowds. Could you stand before a room full of students eager to hang on your every word?" she asked.

"There is a difference between a crowd and an audience. You can become lost in a throng. However, an audience is there for *you*, validating what you have to say. Everyone is focused and interested. There's not much personal interaction, which suits my purposes. Regardless, to know you can make a difference in others' lives, I cannot imagine anything finer than teaching."

Phil leaned in close. He caught another waft of lavender. "Would it be terrible if I asked for another kiss?" she whispered.

Without hesitating, Spencer pulled her across his lap, his shaft hardening at the contact. He curled her in close to his chest and kissed her thoroughly.

God, the taste of her.

Closing his eyes, he savored the flavor like molten honey. He could not get enough. Several minutes passed.

"Kiss me here, Spence."

His eyes opened. Phil had unbuttoned her gown to her waist, and her chemise pulled down to show a vast expanse of creamy, lush cleavage. He could not stop the groan from leaving his throat.

"Explore, touch my breasts. Put your mouth on them," she urged.

A woman's breasts never held any fascination for him. Until tonight. His brothers and friends seemed enamored of them as they spoke of them enough. Now he understood what they had meant. Pulling on her chemise, he ripped it, and Phil laughed throatily in response.

Spencer halted. What if he made a hash of this seduction, which seemed to be progressing of its own accord? She instructed a professor who knew nothing about the carnal acts between a man and a woman except what his older brothers had shared with him over the years. More than a few of their exploits were blush-inducing, and he often wondered if they exaggerated the salacious content to see if they could shock him.

Glancing down, he caught the steady gaze of her tea-brown eyes. Did he notice something swimming in their depths? Did he catch of glimpse of what he surmised could be a prostitute's seduction? Phil studied him as if awaiting his next move. Queasiness moved through him, mixed with an unease that stoked his annoyance. Old doubts and insecurities overwhelmed everything he'd been feeling.

The passion that roared through him dissolved in a heartbeat. All this reeked with the distinct odor of mendacity. How easily he'd forgotten her profession and why she came here in the first place. Spencer clutched the torn cloth of her chemise and covered her exposed breasts.

Phil's brows furrowed in confusion. "What is it?"

Spencer pushed her away until she sat upright. "I am not a man who wishes to be trifled with. You were hired to do a job, and I must say thus far, you have performed most ably and shown yourself to be highly skilled. I commend you."

"Perform?" Phil gasped. The confused look on her face turned to anger. "How dare you?" Living flame cracked to life in her narrowed eyes.

Her flash of temper would not cow him. "You were paid to provide a service. I am merely an assignment, a task to be completed as you await transport away from here. I should have stayed firm in my original conviction on this matter. Why did you take the job? Surely you had harlots aplenty you could have sent in your stead?"

Huffing, Phil reached for the nearby blanket and wrapped it around her shoulders. The simmering rage that lurked within burst forth.

"For a supposedly educated man, you are quite stupid," Phil snapped. "Why did I take this job? I wanted to escape my brothel prison for a few days. I figured a thirty-year-old aristocrat virgin, which in itself is rather pathetic, wouldn't notice my lack of enjoyment in the act. To be blunt, I wanted the money. Your friends paid a tidy sum. I wanted it all for myself." Phil scrambled to her feet, and he did as well. His erection deflated; his burning passion was reduced to ash.

"Yes. Pathetic. It's a term I am very familiar with. Women have tossed the word at me before. Why should you be any different? Let us say here and now that your contract is fulfilled. You have earned your coin. I think it wise we try and avoid each other for the rest of your stay." He gave her a stiff and formal bow. "Goodnight, *madam.*"

Spencer placed deliberate emphasis on the last word. How could he have forgotten that salient fact? She sold sex for profit and laid with men for money. He'd allowed his long-buried emotions to come out of hiding, and because of it, he believed that more existed between them.

Never again.

He stalked from the room, then slammed the door behind him.

Chapter 10

AN HOUR LATER, AND an aching disappointment still twisted Phil's insides. Devil take it; his words bloody hurt. She'd retired to her dusty room and now sat before the fire, wearing her woolen nightgown, replaying the incident downstairs. Curling her bare feet under the garment, she watched the flames dance and sputter in the hearth.

Perhaps she should not have called him pathetic, but how dare he call what passed between them these last two days a performance?

What did I do or say to have him become so angry?

Phil stopped thinking of this as an "assignment" or "job" from the first time she'd heard his luxurious, velvet voice. It solidified after she shaved him and revealed the beguiling face underneath the spectacles and facial hair. The feeling grew the more they conversed and shared confidences.

Spence no longer wore the glasses in her presence. Phil found his lack of guile fascinating and sweet. His innocence touched a part of her heart she thought would never be breached.

How to make him understand?

Why bother?

Even if they followed through on the feelings bubbling between them, nothing could ever come of it. Spence was the refined third son of a duke with straightforward plans for an academic career.

How could a prossie fit into that world?

She couldn't—not ever.

A crash sounded from his room next door, followed by a colorful curse. Enough of brooding and nursing hurt feelings, she rose and moved toward the connecting door. Was it locked? Phil turned the handle and slipped in. Spence faced the fireplace, his hands gripping the mantel, his head bent as if deep in thought.

"Go away, Miss McGrattan." His voice was weary and distant.

"No, I won't. Do you think me unfeeling, so crafty in my machinations that I would reveal deep parts of my past to elicit a response from you? Or did you think I made up the whole sordid incident? That every word I spoke was a lie? Do you think me such an automaton? That I felt nothing when you kissed me? When you touched me?"

She took a step closer. "You're the *only* man in all these wretched years that has made me feel anything! There, a confession. You made a madam *feel*. Not many men can lay claim to that. Be proud of your accomplishment. Savor it. Brag to your brothers and friends that you brought a prossie to her knees in surrender from the sound of your voice alone!" Phil was yelling now, her voice alive with conflicting emotions like anger, doubt, and compassion.

Phil dashed away a tear from her flushed cheek. "I'm not ashamed of what I feel, nor will I deny it. If you wish me to stay in my room the rest of the week, say so now, and let's be done with it. Stop doubting yourself. Yes, you're inexperienced. Did you not stop to consider that I find that endearing? I'm sorry I said pathetic. God, I could rip out my bloody tongue."

Spence turned and strode toward her. Cupping her cheeks, he leaned in and nuzzled her neck, his warm breath feathering across her sensitive skin. "Forgive me. Absolve this lonely, sad man with no confidence in himself and whose eyes did not see or whose ears did not hear. Who let past experiences cloud what's between us, and with no idea how to deal with the innumerable emotions passing through him? I didn't trust you; I didn't trust myself. Forgive me."

He rested his forehead against hers, and a great sob left her throat. They were in each other's arms, embracing tight, sharing their heat and regrets.

"Oh, Spence. What happens now?"

He tucked her head under his chin, stroking her hair. "We take pleasure in what little time we have. As you said, we take the journey together. Do you forgive me?"

Phil burrowed closer to the hard warmth of his chest. "Yes. Can you forgive *me*?"

"Yes. I've borne humiliation all my life. I could not abide more. I lashed out to protect myself."

Phil held him tighter. "I would *never* hurt you. As I said, I've not lied to you, Spence. Not once."

"I know. Will you come and lay with me? I wish to hold you for a while. Nothing more."

Curling up next to him, she gloried in the feather softness of the bed in contrast to the sturdiness of his body. How comforting to lie in his embrace. Resuming their physical explorations tonight wasn't appropriate, but she did have a few questions.

"You speak of past humiliations, in what way? You told me of the girl at the party."

He stroked her arm. "You don't want to hear this."

"I do, Spence. It made you into the man you are today."

He chuckled, the melodic tone sparking her nerve endings. "You mean a shy hermit who avoids civilization, preferring the company of dogs and books over human contact? There were many incidents. I was entirely out of my element when I was sent away to school at twelve. I need some order in my life and a familiarity with my surroundings. No one in my family truly understood this, nor could I properly explain it."

A broken sigh escaped his throat. "Thankfully, my brothers, Harrison and Tremain, were also at the same school. They did their best to protect me from the worst of the bullying. One horrific incident had me bent over a chair with my breeches pulled to my knees. The older lads had already caned me. Now came the ultimate disgrace. I was about to be violated by either one of them or an inanimate object. I do not know what would have been worse. I was at school barely a month."

A lump formed in her throat. Sorrow for his childhood traumas swamped her, causing her eyes to grow moist.

"That's terrible. What happened?" she whispered.

"Tremain, older than me by one year, stepped into the room. He fought them off. How embarrassing to be found in such a vulnerable position. My brother helped me right my clothes and wiped the tears from my cheek. We never spoke of the episode again. To this day, Tremain is not only my brother but my good friend. Same with Harrison, the oldest."

He stared off toward the room's opposite side, his expression haunted. "I found myself in other awkward situations during the next couple of years, but nothing as mortifying as the one I've described. I could have screamed and cried and demanded to be sent home. However, Tremain said to hold my head high and not to show fear. I followed his wise advice. And with each additional incident, I withdrew even more than I normally did. I hid my emotions. It became part of who I am. I don't understand it, but I've revealed more to you these last few days than I have to anyone, including my family."

Why did life have to be so bloody hard?

Even those with wealth and privilege struggled to survive. Perhaps Spence had the right of it, hiding away from society and pursuing his passion for research and history. The shocking thing? She quickly could join him in this self-imposed isolation. What a wonderful dream. One that could never come true. But why not enjoy these brief moments together, as he said?

"Spence, I know you don't want my sympathy, but I'm sorry you were exposed to such cruelty. The world is a harsh place. For a time, let us leave it behind us."

"Will you stay? Sleep in my arms? All night? Please, Phil."
The softly spoken words melted her heart. "Yes. I will."

Chapter 11

LIGHT FILTERED THROUGH the draperies giving enough illumination for Phil to realize it was morning. She was alone in the large bed. Lord, she'd slept in her clothes. Yawning, she stood, smoothed her gown, and went downstairs. The door to the study was open, and without thinking, she stepped across the threshold. Both dogs were lying in front of the hearth. Justinian gave her a welcoming woof as she scanned the room's interior. No professor.

The clock in the corner bonged nine times. She'd slept deep and long, one of her more restful slumbers—ever. Curled up in a man's warm embrace and not used to it at all. But it showed how much she trusted Spence.

Strange, that.

Glancing out the window, Phil sighed. It had snowed overnight, and because of it, she could be stuck here longer than a week. Somehow, the prospect was not as disconcerting as before.

In all these years, she never actually slept with a man. She rather liked it.

Bloody hell, she loved it.

There was something to be said for cuddling together under the blankets and sharing warmth and comfort. She reached for the apron hanging on the peg outside the kitchen door and tied it in place. The sound of splashing water halted her movements.

Spence, taking a bath.

He hummed, the deep tones resonating like the bass string section of an orchestra. Phil stepped into the room, and he stopped in mid-scrub. Spence possessed a lean musculature that she found attractive. Everything about him spoke of elegance. Yes, his nose was a bit long, as were his arms and legs, and his ears stuck out. Regardless of all that, he moved with a poetic fluidity. His eyes and lips were perfection. Phil drank in the vision of his broad shoulders and fine chest. So early in the morning, yet arousal clutched her tight.

As she sat beside the tub, Phil snatched the cloth from his hand. "I'll wash your back. Lean forward."

Muscle moved under the skin and stretched across his shoulder blades. She should not be touching him, but she could not help herself. It became an automatic response, like breathing in and out.

"And what are your plans today?" Spence asked as she trailed the cloth along his spine.

"Breakfast first, of course. I may read later this afternoon while enjoying a cup of tea. I brought a Gothic novel with me." Phil rolled the cloth lower, across the top of his fine arse. "Then I suppose after dinner, I'll come to your bed. Lay you flat and straddle your hips. Ride you until you come."

The mere touch of his skin tore down the barriers she kept around her heart. And she should not be talking like this, but the professor said he wanted to learn. "Or perhaps we will move more slowly. Explore each other first."

With the quickness of a predatory animal, Spence clasped the back of her neck, pulled her down until her face was level with his own, and kissed her savagely. How fiercely he possessed her mouth, not giving her quarter. Deeper he plunged until they both panted. She pulled away and dared a glance. His stiff cock could not be missed.

"Why wait?" he growled sensually.

"Oh, Professor. I believe I've created a monster," she teased.

The spell broke as if he realized what he had done. Blinking rapidly, he reached for the nearby towel.

"I *am* sorry." He stood and wrapped it around his waist, the soapy water sluicing across his taut muscles.

"I wasn't complaining, Spence. Far from it. I shouldn't tease so early in the morning, at least not before our tea." Phil gave him a playful wink, hoping to lessen his obvious discomfort.

He awkwardly gathered his clothes in a haphazard bundle and held them before his chest. "Nevertheless, I will leave you to your tasks."

He slipped from the room. How adorable his embarrassment was. He charmed her, aroused her, and she could not wait until the sun set tonight. The lessons would begin in earnest, and Spence would be the pupil and her—the professor.

SPENCER DRESSED AND waited in his room until his erection dissipated. Good God, perhaps she *did* create a monster. What possessed him to act in such a way in the clear light of day? Kissing her lasciviously like a randy beast? His brothers claimed a healthy sex drive ignited passions, deepening them. Perhaps such a thing could be hereditary.

What nonsense.

Phil had been here less than three days, and already his world was turned on its axis. Not handling his emotions upset his equilibrium and disturbed his inner balance. Shouldn't he be more distressed over the prospect? Seeking solitude is how he dealt with such disturbances in the past, but he didn't want to be alone—at least while Phil was here.

Infatuated.

There was no other word to describe his actions. He'd fallen completely and utterly under her spell. Shaking the revelation from his mind, he headed toward the dining room. Upon entering, the odor of ham and eggs inundated his senses. He could become very used to sharing a meal.

Don't. She's leaving the first chance she gets. Do not become attached.

The warning tolled over and over in his head. Accepting it, he stored it in his categorized memory to recall when needed. Spencer sat at the table as she poured his tea, giving him a sunny smile that told him it was already too late. The attachment was firmly in place—on his end, at least.

Phil sat opposite. "Did you see the snow? Obviously, since you cleared a path to the outside privy. Thank you for that, by the by." She cut into her egg.

Her chatter was adorable. It warmed his heart. The revelation was astonishing, as he could never stand mindless prattle from people.

"Do you think this snowfall will hamper the old man's travels? Boyle, you said his name was? No matter, we have enough food." She ate part of the fried egg and bit into her toast. "Spence, the night after next will be New Year's Eve, can you imagine? 1882. We must celebrate and ring in the new. I believe there is another bottle of wine in the root cellar. I'll roast a chicken; there was one in your grocery order. A fancy New Year's Eve meal will be just the ticket."

Phil sipped her tea. "Though my idea of a fancy meal may completely differ from what *you* consider a fancy meal. Anyway, there are vegetables aplenty to prepare."

Spencer murmured agreement as he ate, keeping his gaze firm on her. How animated and bright she was this morning. He envied her joy in simple things like planning meals and discussing the new year.

"I've been wondering about a few things," she continued, "When I first came upon you in your study that first day, you walked in a stooped position to reach for papers from the bookcase. I must say I was worried that you suffered from a curvature of the spine until you walked into the dining room for supper straight as a broom handle. I have to ask—why?"

Spencer shrugged. "It's a simple question of economy of movement. I have improved my workday efficiency by several minutes by not straightening upright every time I leave my desk."

"And I suppose that extends to shaving as well?"

"Quite so."

Phil chuckled as she nibbled on her toast. "How can you live in this barren, lonely place without transport? What if something happened?"

"You mean, what if I sliced my finger on a piece of paper?" He popped a piece of ham into his mouth, keeping his gaze on her.

"A paper cut can bloody well hurt, and what if it became infected? What if you fell off the edge of the cliff? Or become seriously ill? Who would look after you, and how would you seek assistance? It would be best if you had a horse at the very least," Phil stated.

"I had a horse up until two months past."

She laid her utensils across her plate and gave him a look of shock. "You did? What happened to the beast?"

"Narses died of a digestive ailment. Luckily, it happened the day before Boyle arrived. I had to pay him a pretty penny to take the unfortunate animal away on his wagon."

Spencer frowned. Though he had stayed up all night with Narses, he didn't know what to do except keep the horse as comfortable as possible until the end. He watched helplessly while the horse writhed with pain in his stall, his stomach distended. He would have put the poor creature out of its misery if he had a revolver. A horrible night indeed.

The worry of sudden illness extended to his dear companions. Theodora was no longer young; arthritis hampered her every move. If something happened to his hounds... He shook the horrid thoughts from his mind.

"I'm sad for the horse, but shouldn't you purchase another right away? It would be best if you were not out here far away from civilization without means of transport. What is this place, anyway? A lodge?"

He was inwardly thrilled over her concern. Perhaps she cared about him. Even if it were only a tiny amount, he would take it.

"Do you worry for me then, Phil?"

"Of course, you daft man. I can't stand the thought of you out here alone." Shaking her head, she sipped her tea. Not only did she reveal plenty with those words, but her look of solicitude also warmed his heart. She truly worried about him. How gratifying.

"I prefer to be alone. It gives me a reprieve from conversation and interaction. I am more in control when I am alone."

"You're having conversations with me. Is it such a chore, then?"

"Not with you," Spencer murmured. "As for the horse, I meant to purchase another, but time slipped away from me. This place belonged to my grandfather. An avid huntsman, he used to come here for the plentiful game before he fell ill. So, it *is* a sort of hunting lodge, I suppose. It has not been used in the twenty-two years since his death. I own it now."

Phil looked aghast. "This is your home?"

"No, I have an estate outside of London near Swanley. Being a son of a duke has its advantages. When I reached the age of majority, I was given Penhaven by my father. One of several manors and properties he owned. I haven't been there in many months but employ a competent steward and a small staff of servants who keeps things running smoothly."

He chuckled as he cut into his ham and popped a piece in his mouth. "My parents know me well. They gifted me the more isolated of the ducal properties. It's up on a hill far enough away from the village to give the illusion of privacy and away from the blasted trains. What a racket they can make...Phil, what's wrong?"

HOW ON EARTH COULD she forget that his father was a duke? It was easy to overlook his pedigree in this grimy place with his disheveled appearance, though his voice and formal mode of speech were a dead giveaway.

Here, Son. You are now a man, have a manor house. Happy birthday and all that rot.

Her heart sunk like a stone thrown into a still lake. Common sense told her there could be nothing between them, but a kernel of hope took root last night despite her feeble protests. A hope that something more permanent could exist between them.

Addlepated, dreamy fool.

Phil frowned, wiped her mouth with the napkin, and tossed it to her plate, her appetite gone. "Nothing. At times I forget the fact you are part of the aristocracy."

Quite beyond my reach.

"I do not consider myself as such. It's Harrison who is the heir apparent, not I. At thirty-three, soon to be thirty-four, he feels pressured to settle down and set up his nursery. Granted, he's placing the pressure on himself."

Spence gulped his tea. "Thank God no such expectations will be thrust upon me. Harrison is the Marquess of Tennington, a courtesy title, but a great deal of responsibility goes with it. The queen recently ennobled him, allowing him to sit in the House of Lords. Even Tremain, as the second son, had expectations forced on him. He joined the army and was made Captain. That left me free to pursue my academic dreams. I am quite fortunate to have been born last."

How foolish to indulge in schoolgirl fantasies. What absolute silliness.

"Yes, how fortunate." The uncontrollable urge to run to her dusty chamber, fling herself upon the bed, and cry her eyes out nearly overcame her. But it wasn't in her nature. Instead, she stood and held her emotions in check. "I have much to do to prepare for tonight's meal." They were having leftover stew, but Phil would use any excuse to make her escape.

He stared at her, his expressive eyes showing confusion, his brows knotted in puzzlement. She tried to keep her voice even and devoid of emotions, but he had apparently heard the coolness in her tone.

"What is it?" he questioned. "What's wrong?"

Spence was attuned to her every mood change, which might not be a good thing at all.

How could Phil explain when she barely comprehended her confused emotions? Or tell him that leaving him would be the hardest thing she would ever do? That she wanted much more between them, but the prospect was impossible. Outside of this small, remote world, they would not mix in society, nor would society accept such a couple.

How utterly depressing.

Instead of succumbing to the distressing thoughts swirling about in her mind, Phil did what she did best, retreated behind a wall of polite indifference. Her place of escape that she had built years before. A safe haven.

Steeling her resolve and shuttering her emotions, she moved to his side, picked up the teapot, and poured him a fresh cup.

"Nothing at all. I'm fine. Drink your tea and get yourself off to your work."

Phil walked out of the room, her knees shaking.

He must never know how deeply she was falling for him.

Chapter 12

THE REST OF THE MORNING, Phil kept occupied by organizing and cleaning the kitchen area. Making it entirely presentable would be impossible, but she wanted it orderly enough to work in. It also kept her mind off painful thoughts.

The professor declined lunch again as she figured he might, thus proving that giving him a hearty breakfast had been a good plan on her part. One she would continue to follow while she was here.

Deciding to take an afternoon break, Phil located a small parlor, but there was no furniture and, unbelievably, more begrimed than the kitchen. Instead, she took a tray laden with hot tea and raspberry cakes to her room. At least there was a fire and a serviceable enough upholstered chair.

The lodge was peaceful. Phil reveled in it. When was the last time she could sit, read, enjoy a cuppa, and relax? It wasn't easy to recall. Using one of her suitcases as a stool, she put her feet up. But the quiet tranquility was soon broken by the sounds of slamming doors and heavy foot treads. Spence was pacing about in his room.

The knob rattled on the connecting door as if he clasped it. Phil waited. Would he enter? Moments passed. Not a sound. Then the door flew open, and Spence stood in the doorway.

"Is something amiss?" she asked.

He muttered under his breath, then said in a louder voice, "I-I was wondering what you planned to serve for dinner tonight."

"Do you have any special requests? I thought we would finish the stew. I could make ham sandwiches as well. Would you prefer something else? There is a portion of mutton."

His concentrated stare caused a thrill of pleasure to trickle along her spine. The blue of his eyes was mesmerizing, such turbulent emotions swirling about in their depths. It was as if he were undressing her with his eyes.

"What I prefer." The questioning words rolled over his tongue with a sensual cadence. "I would prefer to be able to concentrate on my work. But I cannot. You fill my thoughts, crowding out everything else."

Phil closed her book, trying not to show how much his frank statement thrilled her. "I do?"

"Yes. You said you have things to teach me." Spence took a step closer.

"And you said you were not averse to learning them. Correct?"

"Correct. What 'things,' exactly?"

"Well, I thought tonight, after supper, we would—explore. Each other. Thoroughly." Her voice dropped an octave, sounding husky to her own ears. Bloody hell, the professor had her in complete knots.

"How thoroughly?" he rasped.

"Words can spark arousal as much as touch. If I go into detail, we will both be breathing hard. Let's say—explore enough to bring you to a climax. But no further. Not tonight. As I said: the anticipation. I thought we would build up to the sex. It's called 'precoital activity.' Then, on New Year's Eve, the act itself. If that meets with your approval."

An almighty heat roared between them. Phil sensed it, and judging by the professor's flushed cheeks, he also felt it.

The wise madam at the brothel in Belfast taught her much about arousal, desire, and emotional intimacy. But Phil never had many opportunities to put all she'd learned to practical use.

Until she met Spencer Hornsby.

"You say *my* climax. What about you?" he asked.

She shrugged. "This isn't about me. I'm here to give *you* pleasure."

Spence sat on the edge of the bed, facing her. "I want to give it in return. Or we will not do this at all."

If she had allowed her vulnerability to show, tears would have formed. But Phil fought them back. When did anyone ever do anything for her, including giving pleasure?

"Spence, there is a chance I may not become aroused enough to... Oh, damn it all," she muttered. How to explain her apprehension about being able to reach an orgasm? "As I said, I've never found true gratification in most of my encounters. Usually, I faked my interest."

His brows furrowed. "One can fake such a response?"

"A woman can. It is easily accomplished. Moaning, heavy breathing, writhing. It often resulted in a nice gratuity."

"I do not wish you to 'fake it' with me," he replied softly. "Can we at least try?"

This man's innocence and wonder made her heart tumble wildly. "We can. But if I cannot—know it's not you."

Spence stood. "After supper, then?"

"Yes," she whispered. "After supper."

Nodding, he turned and departed, no doubt returning to his study. Trying to remain detached would be problematic, but Phil must protect her fragile heart.

Blast it all.

She could admit the truth. It *was* fragile. Her logical side dismissed the fact of their mutual attraction. They've only known each other for a few days. Impossible to form a bond in such a short time.

Or was it?

SUPPER PASSED QUICKLY enough, but Spencer didn't taste a blasted thing. When they finished, they quietly ascended the stairs to his room.

What to do? Kiss her? Touch? Speak tender words? Wasn't that all part of the precoital activity she'd spoken of?

The questions were answered when Phil moved her hand across the fall of his trousers, and he immediately hardened.

"Let us give each other—gratification," she whispered.

Every nerve ending in his body sparked to life. Spencer had no idea if this reaction could be construed as usual. Perhaps it was the fact that he remained a virgin. Could any woman's attentions have him reacting so swiftly? Somehow, he doubted it.

Years before, he had a revealing conversation with his oldest brother, Harrison. Harry certainly indulged in female company in his early twenties. Not certain if he still did. His brother confided that most of the experiences were empty and meaningless, a way to satisfy his youthful libido. Spence concluded that sex must be a cold and empty task, which made him all the more determined to avoid it.

But *this.*

Phil slid her delicate hand across his crotch purposefully, and he hardened further. His breathing grew ragged, his excitement on the edge of losing control. A low, savage sound rumbled deep in his chest.

"I will confide, Spence. Thanks to my circumstances, I became determined not to end up a bunter, which is a prostitute who begs, ruts, and survives on the streets. If I were to do this, it would be on *my* terms, like dictating the type of sex, carefully choosing my customers, and placing a time limit on my services. It's a business, nothing more."

Phil squeezed him, and he groaned in response.

"It is a rather intimate business," he rasped.

She moved her hand away. Already he missed her touch. "To some, not to me."

"Are you saying you felt nothing in *all* your assignations?"

"Most men do not last more than a few minutes, which is fine by me. But I've encountered a rare few with the stamina to last an hour or more. In those instances, I came close to experiencing some pleasure. But it remained a fleeting ghost of a response."

"How is that possible? The stamina, I mean."

"A wise woman told me once that in matters of sex, the mind plays a large role. You can learn to control your physical responses."

"Is that what you did? Learn to shut out pleasure?"

She paused as if contemplating what he said. "Yes, I suppose so."

Spencer cupped her cheek, brushing his thumb across her lower lip. "And are you doing it now?"

Phil covered his hand with hers and gazed into his eyes. Her look softened. "No. Not with you."

That heartfelt confession made his chest puff out with masculine pride. It also touched the depths of his soul. Try as he might, he could not close himself off from Philomena McGrattan, nor did he want to. "Can you show me and teach me how to—last?"

A sly, sensual smile curved about her mouth. "Yes. Let's move to your bed."

Once they lay on it, she unbuttoned his trousers and pulled them and his smalls past his hips. She sat back and examined him as if it were a specimen in a laboratory. "There is no correlation between size and performance, you know. The customer I told you about with the stamina? His cock was insignificant in length and girth, but he knew how to wield it."

"You talk as if he were a sword."

She chuckled. "Well, swords and sheaths are terms frequently used regarding sex." Phil gripped his shaft tight, and his body trembled in response. "A decent width. Most women do like the feeling of a man inside her, filling and stretching her. To me, width is more important than length, but that is only my opinion."

Good God, they were lying in his bed discussing the mechanics of the most private part of him. Mortifying, perhaps, but also fascinating.

Phil gripped him tighter. "A good length as well, Professor."

"I am gratified to hear it," he said through clenched teeth. Honestly, he was ready to blow apart.

Control. Concentrate.

"Now, I want you to tell me when you're on the precipice of ecstasy."

"I'm there now," he moaned.

Her sensual laugh trickled down his spine as cooling drops from a spring rain. "The idea is to bring you to the very edge, then cease. Have your mind control your need to climax. Clench inwardly. That also works, I'm told."

Phil started unhurriedly by rolling her hand back and forth until the swollen head peeked out of his foreskin. She increased the pace and pressure of her grip. Like any youth, he often masturbated. Not much of late, and it was never as wonderful as this.

The pressure built in his bollocks; his breathing ragged. "Stop!" he panted.

I'm close to spilling.

Phil released him. "There. Take deep breaths. In a few minutes, we shall try again."

"Vixen. You are taking pleasure from tormenting me."

"Perhaps a little. Spence, I believe you will turn out to be an amazing lover."

"And when will we test that theory, later tonight?"

Pray, let it be so.

He had never wanted to be inside a woman as much as this moment.

She shook her head, her shining, golden-red hair falling about her shoulders. "Not tonight, but New Year's Eve, remember? This cannot be rushed. After I bring you to your release, can we try...with me?" Phil sounded tentative and shy in her request.

"Anything," he croaked, his voice hoarse. On that note, she clutched him again and stroked. When she cupped his bollocks, he nearly came out of his skin. His insides were aflame, burning with an almighty heat as if he would combust from within.

Spencer clenched as instructed, biting on his bottom lip and tasting blood. His voice grew rough from the groans, demanding she move faster and grip him tighter. How many minutes passed? Who knows, as he lost all sense of time and place.

"That's it. Come for me, Spence."

He yelled her name as he climaxed, his body wracked with wave after wave of desire. His hips lifted off the bed with each shudder. It went on for many minutes. Spencer closed his hand over hers. Finally, the tremors subsided, and his breathing returned to normal. By God, he never felt more alive.

"Well. That was bloody intense," Phil murmured.

"There's...there's a handkerchief in my trousers pocket."

Phil found it and cleaned them up. Tossing it on the end table, she curled in next to him. Spencer didn't even bother to pull up his trousers.

"See? The longer you can hold out, the more forceful the release. Rest a moment," she crooned.

Intense did not begin to describe it. Every nerve ending tingled with awareness, every sense heightened. A mixture of their scents lingered in the room, along with a muskier, earthy odor that was not at all unpleasant. Colors were more vivid, and the nearness of Phil ignited his skin. Savoring the sensations for several minutes, he wound stray locks of her silken hair around his fingers.

"Do you wish me to stroke you?" he asked.

PHIL MOVED IN CLOSER, cuddling up next to his comforting warmth. Imagine her acting as if she had all the answers to everything carnal. She didn't, not even close. She went through the motions for years, allowing only two positions: missionary and her on top. In time, she became adept at performing.

Most men hardly noticed, or perhaps they didn't care. Phil remained aloof in her sexual dealings, often increasing the man's passion. Once in a while, she rewarded a select few with her finely honed and rehearsed response.

Deceiving Spence was off the table.

Deep down, she longed to experience genuine desire, but she was also worried she wouldn't respond to him as she wished to.

Phil tunneled her fingers through his chest hair. "We should begin the next phase." Sitting upright, she pulled her nightgown up to her waist, bent her legs, and spread them wide. "Here, Professor. Make a study of me."

Spence pulled his trousers up over his hips and kneeled between her thighs. He leaned in and examined her. She couldn't help but laugh at his serious expression.

"You're wet. That is a decided benefit, correct?" he questioned.

"Yes. And for me, rare. In the past, I used lubricants to ease a man inside me."

"Ah. The wetness allows for effortless entry for both the man and the woman. How fascinating."

"All I have to do is touch you, hear that splendid voice, and I grow wet with need. Only you, Spence, and I'm amazed as much as I am terrified." She clutched his arm briefly, giving it a reassuring squeeze.

He sat upright, his brows knotting together. "For God's sake, why?"

"I don't want to bloody well feel anything," she whispered.

Reaching between her legs, Spence trailed his fingers upward, leaving a path of heat in its wake. "We're alone here, Phil. Two people are giving each other pleasure. No boundaries and no promises. An unknown journey. An exploration. I will leave doubt behind if you leave your fright."

God, his voice.

Smooth as silk and deep as sin, each syllable playing havoc with her restraint. She nodded. "All right. You have a deal, Professor Hornsby."

"My oldest brother, Harry, told me there is a special button hidden under a hood of skin that can give a woman extreme pleasure." He explored, causing her to shudder with each caress. "Ah, there. For once, he did not exaggerate."

He rubbed vigorously, causing her to moan softly. "How inexperienced are you?" Phil gasped.

"No experience at all, but I have two older brothers who boasted of their erotic tales in excruciating detail. They mentioned things I would like to try." The corner of his mouth turned upward in a playful, sensual smile. A smile she had never seen him use before. How it appealed.

Dare she ask? Spence was not what she imagined he would be. Tentative and shy initially, he seemed to take to this as a duck to water. If he could brush aside his suspicions and doubts, then she could, too.

"Like what, Professor?"

"Against the wall, on a table, me behind, sitting in a chair—" He rattled off a few more positions, and with each one, he increased the rhythm. "Tremain is fond of oral sex. Perhaps that would be something to try." Leaning in, he pushed one finger inside her, causing her to moan. He thrust in and out, rubbing his thumb against the hardened, sensitive nub. "Your mouth on my cock, my tongue plunged into your—"

She gasped, a ragged moan escaping her lips. Colors swirled in her vision.

Bloody hell, an orgasm.

All from his mere touch.

And Spence, ever the scholarly man, used his voice to bring her pleasure. *Such* pleasure. Phil's heart banged against her ribcage.

Heaving, she dared to meet his gaze. The look on his face was not arrogance, smug in the knowledge that he gave her pleasure as no man had before. Instead, she read tenderness in his thoughtful expression, making her insides tumble with yearning.

With a slow gentleness, he lowered her nightgown, brushed her matted hair off her forehead, and kissed her tenderly. He lay prone and brought her with him, covering them with his bedspread.

"Sleep here in my arms again. All night. Please, Phil. Say yes."

The depth of intimacy between them, physical and emotional, astounded her. A rush of elation flooded her.

Oh, bloody hell.

It's true; she didn't imagine it after all. She *was* falling for him—and taking leave of her senses.

The voice inside her whispered urgently, *"Go back to your room. Keep your distance from this man. Guard your heart."*

It was too late—all of it.

Instead of running, she nestled in close and nodded, powerless to resist him. She would save all her resolve until it was time to go. It would require every ounce of it to leave him.

Until then, Phil knew she was lost.

Chapter 13

NEW YEAR'S EVE

THE PAST FORTY-EIGHT hours passed in a blissful, sensual blur. Last night was spent much as the night before. Touching, caressing, and kissing every inch of her skin and learning just how sensitive a woman's breasts can be. It was arousing to have a woman kiss and explore every part of his body. But tonight would be different.

First, Spencer decided after an afternoon of burying himself in research and seeing to the dogs' comfort; he should pay a little attention to his own needs—and his appearance.

Unfortunately, he didn't bring any formal clothing. Whom would he dress for, the hounds? However, there was one pair of black trousers, a decent white shirt, and a white cravat he could use in a pinch. The gold waistcoat was not in the best shape, sporting many frayed threads. It was in better condition than his black one and more fitting for a special dinner. As far as a coat, he would forgo such, as the brown tweed wouldn't match the rest of his garments.

Spencer snipped away as many loose threads as he could. Old habits die hard with regard to the current culture's standards and mode of dress, even though he personally couldn't give a toss. When he came of age, he refused the offer of a valet, for he was capable enough of looking after himself. He preferred it.

One positive experience from attending school: learning to stand on his own two feet—to an extent. And there was the fact that the thought of someone handling his belongings upset him. Notwithstanding, Spencer wanted to look his level best tonight.

Concentrating on the task at hand proved problematic, for the anticipation of sex would not leave his mind. While nervous, he looked forward to consummating the intimacy that had grown between them. The proof lay in the way his hand shook as he gripped the scissors. Would it be as cold, mechanical, and meaningless as his brothers hinted? Or as Phil experienced? Granted, Tremain and Harry said not all their experiences left them feeling empty. A select few were quite memorable.

Spencer hoped his first time would be—unforgettable. Now that he thought about it, his brothers' bragging *was* exaggerated. Though they described their sexual exploits in salacious detail, he now understood that they were giving him instruction, preparing him so he would not act as a bumbling fool if and when he ever decided to embark on an affair.

His memory had always been sharp, and his organizational skills marveled many. He could retain vast amounts of information, which would be helpful for the task ahead. Only this wasn't a task to him.

It meant *everything.*

Philomena McGrattan inflamed him as no other woman before. He would not have agreed to this if he didn't already have deep feelings for her. How could it be possible after several days of acquaintance?

Apparently, it was possible, and Spencer would not deny or dismiss it. *Something* existed between them. Phil admitted it as well. Perhaps they would both exorcize the attraction from their systems tonight. Or sex could merely fan the simmering embers into a roaring blaze.

Spencer placed the scissors on the table and inspected the gold waistcoat. It would have to do. Now to freshen up. Should he shave? He sported the barest hint of a beard, and Phil said she liked it. No, he would leave it for now. If it made him appear a little rakish in her eyes, all the better, he could use all the assistance he could get.

A hunger he could not describe thrummed through him. The walls he had erected around his heart were all but smashed, but enough of the protective barrier existed to absorb any coming heartache and disappointment. For his sanity, he hoped an adequate amount remained. Spencer believed it would be prudent for him to plan for any number of scenarios.

But not tonight.

He wanted to focus on Phil only. Tucking the garment under his arm, he headed for his small dressing room.

Nothing prepared Spencer for the beautiful vision awaiting him in the dining room. Phil wore a gold silk gown with gold embroidered roses as the design. Lace was abundant across the bodice, revealing her amazing cleavage. Spencer swallowed hard. Arousal held him in thrall but also an ardent tenderness. The gown was not overtly daring but beautiful and appropriate for a holiday meal.

Her hair was left down, flowing past her shoulders, a few locks held in place by silver combs, her beautiful face on full display. She wore very little makeup, and he preferred her fresh-faced prettiness. Collecting his thoughts, he stepped forward and bowed. She curtsied.

"Too bad I didn't bring gloves and a fan. Spence, you look very dashing." Phil caressed his cheek, her fingers lingering on his whiskers. "Take my advice. Never grow a bushy beard again. These cheekbones should not be hidden. It would be a mortal sin."

He clasped her hand, raised it to his lips, and kissed it. Phil smiled, her eyelashes fluttering.

"Now," she turned around, showing the back of her gown. It was cut low, showing the delicate curve of her shoulders. "The gown hooks up the front, but I need your assistance tying the bow. Would you?"

Though his hands shook, he managed to do as she asked. About to kiss the curve of her neck, he halted.

Do not rush. Anticipation.

Instead, Spencer escorted her to her chair and gallantly pulled it out for her. She flushed in what he hoped was pleasure at the gesture.

"I hope you don't mind. I ladled out the food in the kitchen. It would be tedious to drag it all up here, including the chicken carcass. If we wish more, we can fetch it later. I could only find one bottle of white wine. Better we save it to ring in the new year. Meanwhile, the claret will do."

Spencer sat opposite. How he adored her chatter. To think days ago, he couldn't abide it. It did not annoy him anymore but instead calmed him. He snapped open the napkin and laid it across his hips. The food on the plate looked appetizing. Sliced roast chicken with bread stuffing, sliced carrots, mashed potatoes, and peas in a creamy sauce. He hadn't enjoyed a meal like this in months since he last visited Gransford Manor. The turkey dinner the housekeeper brought him on Christmas Day did not compare to this feast.

It appealed all the more because Phil prepared it. She could bring him a bowl of watery gruel, and he would think it incredible. Yes, he was entirely smitten.

"You've outdone yourself, Phil. You quite sparkle tonight. Everything is perfection, from the food to you. Your beauty overwhelms me."

She blushed prettily. "Oh, my. You do know how to charm."

"No, I do not. Not at all. It's *you* that brings this out of me. Only you."

Phil blinked several times as if having difficulty processing his declaration. He meant it.

"Oh, Spence," she whispered.

Raising his glass, he said, "To us and this night. To you, my dear Phil. 'She walks in beauty like the night. Of cloudless climes and starry skies, and all that's best of dark and bright, meet in her aspect and her eyes.' And I cannot believe I just quoted Byron." Spencer took a sip and shook his head with amusement.

Phil's eyes were moist. Perhaps he did right to quote maudlin poetry. They tucked into their meals. All that could be heard was the crackling of the wood in the fireplace. The silence did not feel awkward but spoke of a peaceful companionship he found consoling.

Spencer watched her under half-hooded eyes as she ate her chicken. Her good manners spoke of her middle-class upbringing, though it had been cut short by her admission. To lose one's parents at such a vulnerable age, he could not imagine.

Spencer adored his parents. Their marriage was not typical of the aristocracy. They loved and respected one another. They spent time together and talked to one another. It's probably why he and his brothers remained unattached. All of them were holding out for true love. Sentimental at its core but nonetheless true. They'd all spoken of it on more than one occasion.

Time was running out for Harry. As the heir, he had an unspoken duty to marry and have children. His brother spoke of it enough. Not long ago, Harry announced that he would begin the bridal hunt immediately. When he turned thirty-four, he would seek a bride amongst the ton. What a cold and calculating endeavor.

Spencer had vowed then and there that he would not marry, but if he did, only the truest and most profound love would induce him because he would not settle for anything less. The option to hold out for it seemed a realistic outlook, unlike poor Harry, for whom time was not a friend and duty a stern taskmaster.

He glanced down at his empty plate. A hunger still burned hot and fierce inside him, but not for more food. No, nor would drink slake the thirst that accompanied the fire. This exquisite melding of agonies, mere heartbeats from ecstasy, was unlike any emotion or desire he had ever experienced —and he wanted more. At this moment, he yearned for something else—the scent and softness of a woman.

More specifically—Philomena McGrattan.

EATING A FULL MEAL while one's stomach fluttered with nervousness proved difficult, but Phil managed it.

Spence's intense and concentrated gaze stayed on her through the repast, and it took all her resolve not to return it. Perhaps a little light-heartedness was in order. She picked up a chicken leg and tossed it to Spence. He started at the sudden movement but caught the meat in his fist.

Phil picked up a wing. "Shall we rip the meat off the bone as we give each other lusty looks across the table like the scene in Fielding's book, *Tom Jones*? Make bawdy talk of legs, thighs, and plump breasts while licking our lips with rapturous delight?"

Spence laughed. Heartily and loud. The resonant sound sent thrilling chills down her spine.

"Food and sex make for compatible companions, you know." She smiled warmly, giving him a teasing wink.

"Has that been your experience, then?"

"Unfortunately, yes. Which do you wish to hear about, the earl who likes to pour honey over the girls, then proceed to lick it off? Or the Royal Navy captain who likes to fuck food as one of the girls lightly paddles his behind?"

Spence's eyes widened. "How does one do, as you so delicately put it? The food aspect?"

"There is a huge bowl full of cream or a fruit pudding, and then he crams his erect...."

Spence raised his hand to silence her. "Dear God. I may never be able to remove that vision from my mind or eye a bowl of syllabub quite the same way again."

Phil laughed. "One can desire food as much as one can desire sex."

"Not within my knowledge."

"Well, my dear Professor, there are other joys in life besides research and study." She gave him a sultry look as she buried her teeth into the chicken wing, slowly pulling off a strip of meat and skin.

Spence followed suit with the leg. The heated stare he gave her caused her heart to flutter madly. Even watching his throat work was a sensual delight. He tossed the leg to his plate.

"I want you, Phil. I want to be inside you. Now." He stood and held out his hand in invitation. His eyes burned with passion. "I want you in my bed. I want to hold you in my arms. Come with me. Come—for me."

Oh, bloody hell. His words.

The moan that left her throat reverberated through her as heat bloomed between her legs. A poignant ache of longing circled her heart. She dropped the chicken. Phil stepped before him and placed her hand in his. Spence threaded his fingers through hers, the touch scorching.

"Yes, to all of it."

Chapter 14

EVERYTHING THAT HAPPENED after those words of longing seemed to have occurred in a dream. Speaking of his deepest yearnings, revealing how thoroughly aroused he was, gave him the courage to act on every complicated emotion rolling through him. Hand in hand, they climbed the stairs. The anticipation tempted him to gather her in his arms and run the rest of the way to his bedroom.

Spencer's shaft and his heart throbbed in unison as if one entity. Maybe they were. Perhaps certain men could separate emotions from the act of sex, but his instincts told him that he could not. He wouldn't even try tonight because he wanted to feel every moan, every slide of their bodies, and every beat of their hearts.

Phil slipped into her room and returned, waving a small cloth bag.

"Sheaths," she murmured, giving him a shy smile.

Of course. Again, his inexperience showed in his lack of responsibility for avoiding pregnancy, or as his brothers had mentioned: "carnal infections."

"As I said, no man has been near me for three years, but even before, I insisted the men be cloaked in a sheath," she explained.

A sharp pain tore through his heart.

How many men?

In all honesty, it was better not to know. With little knowledge of women and sex, he could allow her statement to make him feel insignificant, merely another inexpert man in a long line of customers. But deep down, he knew that was not the case between them. They were *not* a prostitute and her client. Real, substantial emotion lay between them.

How far and how deep? Time to investigate the possibilities.

They stood before each other. The room's warmth made him thankful he'd lit the fire before going downstairs to dinner. Before they departed the dining room, Spencer had placed the screen in front of the hearth. He assured Phil they would snack on leftovers later in the evening as he planned on working up an appetite.

Spencer cupped her cheeks. So beautiful. Gazing into her eyes, he read doubt. If she looked deep enough, she would also see it in his. Her admission that she had never received any enjoyment should have him worrying further about his upcoming performance. All it did was make him more determined to give her as much pleasure as she could stand.

Spencer embraced her and rested his head on her shoulder, then laid hot kisses on her neck and across her exposed shoulder blades as he yearned to do before dinner. He kissed her forehead, a chaste kiss, but one to calm and reassure her. And perhaps to boost his confidence. With her back to him, he moved his hands to her bare shoulders and down her arms. A whisper of a sigh escaped her lips, and she leaned against his chest.

"Tell me, Spence," she said breathlessly. "What position would you like to try?"

That is a good question.

"What you described that morning you walked in on me taking a bath. Laying me flat on the bed while you—ride me." How amazing that with her, he could reveal his hidden desires. And they burnt with an almighty flame.

"Oh. Bloody hell." Phil turned to face him. "Unhook me here. And hurry," she demanded.

He chuckled but did not rush. The gold gown pooled at her feet in a silken puddle when he reached the last one. A desirous groan left his throat. She wore a corset that matched the shade of the gown. Lace and small bows decorated it along the neckline and down the sides. Matching sheer stockings completed the look. The corset hooked in the front, pushing her glorious breasts together in invitation.

Spencer fell to his knees. How could he not? Phil was a goddess, and how he yearned to worship her. No petticoats or chemise; they were not needed. She kicked off her slippers. Her feet were small and delicate, with an attractive arch. Spencer trailed his hands up her legs, reveling in the silky feel of the stockings.

Phil moaned and placed one leg over his shoulder. Dear God. She lay open for him. The corset had no barrier. He curled his arm about her leg to hold her steady.

A voice inside his head spurned him forward: *kiss and taste every part of her.*

The first licks were tentative and hesitant as he had no clue how to do this. Perhaps if he sucked on that hard, little nub he found before. No wonder Tremain enjoyed this. Banishing his doubt, he dove in, and his tongue plunged into the very heat of her.

"Spence!"

Her joyous cry fueled his ardor. Finding the nub, he bit it gently, then flicked his tongue across it quickly. Phil tunneled her hand through his hair, grabbed a fistful, and pulled with each moan. Her breathing grew shallow and ragged as she neared her peak. Spencer glanced up. Her passionate response encouraged him to continue. Her husky moans demanded it.

They locked gazes, and the intense desire in her eyes shot straight to his soul. By God, he was aroused. She tasted sweet, enticing as a decadent dessert. Phil cried out. Bracing his hands on her slim waist, he pushed to his feet and gathered her into his embrace as she shuddered with her release. His heart soared as he rode the wave of desire with her.

"Spence," she whispered breathlessly. "I've never...hell. Thank you."

He held her tight, his heart beating as fast as hers. Exhaling, Phil stepped back and reached for his cravat, then slowly divested him of his waistcoat and shirt. Laying her hands flat against his bare chest, her eyes met his.

"I've never wanted a man as much as I do you, Spence. Do you find that hard to believe? A jaded whore who prided herself on feeling nothing came apart under your tongue."

Spencer cupped her face, tilting it up to meet his gaze. "Do not refer to yourself as a whore ever again, not in my hearing. You are my Phil. *Mine*. And I am yours," he said fiercely, then kissed her hard, possessing and claiming her. A slight pause, then she met his kiss. They moved toward the bed, not breaking the heated connection between them.

At last, Phil reached for the fall of his trousers. He kicked off his shoes. With a swift jerk, she pulled the garments to the floor, and he stepped out of them, then kicked the clothes aside. Exposed and vulnerable, he stood before her. He also ached for *her* in his heart and soul. The physical evidence of his desire was not hard to miss, and he didn't bother hiding the overwhelming emotions. Lust, desire, a passion so devastating it caused him to tremble. The soft brush of her fingers explored his stomach, following the curve of his hipbones to grip his rigid shaft.

After a few strokes, Phil led him to the bed and motioned for him to lie down. His gaze remained firmly on her, watching in fascination and curiosity as she fit a sheath over him. Straddling his hips, Phil unhooked her corset enough to allow her ample breasts to spill out. Her wet core caressed his cock, causing it to harden further. She squeezed her breasts together and rubbed her nipples until he moaned huskily at the sensual sight.

Spencer pulled her toward him and clamped his mouth on the pebbled nipple. Phil trembled, whispering words of encouragement. He feasted on one, then the other, and strange sensations tore through him. Phil clasped his shaft and rose above it.

God, how he wanted her.

Wet heat encased him. He held her hips still although he ached to raise his. Instead, he waited and allowed her to take the lead. Fully seated, she splayed her hands on his chest.

"Feel that? We are joined. I can feel the beat of your heart between my legs," Phil murmured.

Utterly earth-shattering.

At this moment, inside her, Spencer knew he would never want any other woman but her. His heart swelled with poignant compassion and the knowledge that he wished to stay like this forever. Perhaps he denied himself carnal pleasures in his past, but it had been worth it to experience this. As she said: joined.

Hearts beating as one.

Yes, only Phil could satisfy his heart, body, and mind. God, it felt glorious. Phil moved her hips slightly, but he held her still.

"Wait. Let me...savor. Remember." Spencer closed his eyes and became utterly lost in the multifaceted but intoxicating emotions rolling through him. The intense feelings threatened to overcome him, but he would sort through them later.

Remember.

Within his complex mind, he created a new room. One that only Phil resided in. It would be private and guarded, and only he would be permitted to access the memories. He would need them for the lonely years ahead.

"Ride me," he demanded.

Phil rocked her hips forward, causing him to moan in surrender. His hands could not stay still as they roamed all over her lovely curves. They tunneled through her shimmering hair, down to caress her breasts, then back again as she rode him with wild abandon. Spencer explored every inch of exposed skin. Faster, she moved, tilting forward slightly to change the angle.

The pressure built; it would not take him long. He willed back his release, wishing her to reach her peak first. Spencer couldn't stay still. He lifted his hips, thrusting upward with each slide.

"Talk to me, Spence. Seduce me with your voice. I beg you."

"God, you're so tight. Have you any idea what you do to me?" he rasped. "How much you...."

Tread carefully, the voice inside his head whispered. *Do not reveal your deepest longings. Not yet.*

"Move me. Arouse me."

He slapped her arse, not too hard, but enough to cause her eyes to widen in surprise. Then she smiled.

"Faster. Come for me," he commanded.

Both of them were covered in perspiration from their exertions. Sitting upright, he clasped the nape of her neck and kissed her deeply, then trailed his lips to her breast. That seemed to do it. Phil cried out as her inner muscles clutched him hard. Her climax rolled over him.

His release hit him like a gale-force wind whipping across a stormy sea. They held each other, shaking with spent passion. When he finally caught his breath, Spencer lay on the bed and brought Phil with him. They were still joined. How he wished they could stay like this for all eternity.

Is it possible?

No. Not at all, and his heart contracted in pain at the thought. She would leave in a couple of days, and that filled him with despair.

Chapter 15

HOW HAS SHE NEVER REACHED such breathtaking heights of pleasure in over fifteen years? Did she hold herself in reserve in those other instances? Yes, obviously. Phil was skilled at erecting barriers between gratification and a contract to be filled. After discussing it with the other girls, she found that several shared her sentiment. A rare one or two of the ladies truly enjoyed their tasks regardless of what man, but most? Sex was a chore. A necessity to procure coins in order to live. A job. Nothing more.

That is not the case here. Not at all.

Now that she experienced such unfettered bliss with Spence, how could she ever return to the only life she knew? Not that she plied her wares any longer. The business of running the brothel kept her busy, and she certainly did not miss the couplings. However, she would miss this. Miss *him*—this private, intelligent, and lonely man who touched the deepest parts of her heart.

Phil exhaled. No. She would not become maudlin. This short interlude could not last. There was no use dwelling on their upcoming parting. It would only depress her utterly, and Phil wanted complete ecstasy to fill her heart tonight. She snuggled in closer, her nose nuzzling the strong column of his neck.

"Oh, Professor. As I surmised, you're an amazing lover," she whispered huskily.

He laughed, the deep rumble reverberating in his chest. "I thank you for the kind words. I passed muster, then, for my first try?"

Though his voice teased, the tone vibrated with a poignant vulnerability. And how that touched her heart.

Phil kissed his cheek. "More than passed. Excelled even."

"Any chance we can have another go?"

"Insatiable man. Rest for a bit. Actually, I'm thirsty. Maybe a little food...."

Spence jumped to his feet. "Say no more. I shall venture forth and obtain what we need." He tore off the sheath, tossed it in the nearby rubbish basket, then stepped into his trousers.

Phil chuckled at his light-hearted mood, rolled over on her stomach, and faced him. "You will find the wine and glasses on the counter in the kitchen. The tray is in the dining room; you will need it to bring us a meal. Oh, do you know where the root cellar is?" He nodded. "Place the leftover food there to keep it from spoiling."

Spence gave her a stunning smile. "Any other orders, my queen?"

She dismissed him airily with her hand. "I cannot think of anything at this moment, but I will let you know if I do."

His laughter followed him out the door. Then he hummed *God Save the Queen* as he descended the stairs.

Phil smiled at his lighthearted teasing, then sobered. She did not lie or exaggerate when she stated he was a fantastic lover. The fact that he would only improve saddened her as she would not be around to observe his progress. For his first try, he certainly deserved a medal.

Lord Spencer Hornsby was not perfect.

But on this night, the last one of 1881, he came as close to utter flawlessness as a man could achieve.

With a stretch of her arms, she rolled out of bed. After stirring the embers to life in the fireplace, she walked to the basin, cleaned up, and fastened the hooks on her corset. She crawled onto the bed, tunneling under the plush quilt.

Spence entered, carrying a tray with wine and food. How dangerously sexy and disheveled he appeared, standing there shirtless, his trousers hanging low on his slim, muscular hips with his brown hair tousled and his blue eyes shimmering with life and passion. Every woman should be waited on by such a glorious man.

A stab of yearning tore through her. How she wanted a loving, caring man to wait on her, see to her every need, and hold her close when she required comfort and warmth.

A friend. A companion. An ardent lover.

Shaking away the unrealistic fantasies, Phil gave him a tremulous smile; no doubt her vulnerability was fully displayed.

Spence placed the tray on the bed. "We should ring in the new year at this very minute." He pointed at the mantel clock. "It's ten o'clock, close enough for a celebration."

"You cannot wait another two hours?"

"Phil, I want to ring in the new by making love to you. At midnight, I will be inside you." He removed the cork on the bottle, poured the wine into the goblets, and passed one to her.

Did he have any clue how incredibly sensual he sounded? He spoke freely from his heart, without any guile or prevarications. Something she was not used to in her dealings with most men. Spence cleared his throat and raised his glass. Phil scrambled out of bed, then held hers up.

"Here's to the bright new year and a fond farewell to the old. Here's to the things that are yet to come and to the memories that we hold." They clinked their glasses together. "A very Happy New Year, Miss Philomena McGrattan."

"And to you, Professor-Lord Hornsby." Her voice was quiet, awed after his charming toast. They sipped the wine, and she was about to take another drink when Spence whisked away the glasses and placed them on the table.

Taking her hand, he spun her around and placed her in front of him in a waltz position.

"Now, we dance." He twirled her about the room in breathtaking sweeping motions. Then, incredibly, he began to sing. Of course, he could sing. How could he not with that incredible voice?

"Should auld acquaintance be forgot and never brought to mind? Should auld acquaintance be forgot, and auld lang syne."

Phil did not know whether to laugh or cry. He sang *Auld Lang Syne* with the cadence and beat of the *Blue Danube* by Strauss.

"One-two-three- *"For Auld lang Syne, my dear, for Auld lang Syne, we'll take a cup of kindness yet, for Auld lang Syne."*

His moves were fluid and graceful. Then he hummed the waltz, slowing the beat until they stopped before the fire. "I had dancing lessons years ago and learned the steps to this piece of music."

The room swirled past her in a rush. She found their waltz more intoxicating than the wine they consumed. Cupping her cheeks, he stared down at her. Indeed, she would melt on the spot. What Phil read in his eyes speared her heart. He cared for her—very much. That knowledge warmed her insides as much as it made them tumble in fright.

"You dance very well, Professor," she whispered.

"Happy New Year, Phil." He kissed her, a gentle touch of his lips, which spoke of the tenderness within. But also—the fire. The passion. So vast it could barely be contained.

Do not cry, you silly woman.

Tears threatened, but she blinked them away. Instead, Phil gently caressed his cheek. "Happy New Year, Spence."

Unfathomable emotions hung between them, too numerous and mysterious to name. Pushing them to the back of her mind, Phil pointed to the tray. "Shall we eat? You brought bread, cheese, sliced cold chicken, and my favorite. Grapes. Come, sit here on the bed."

Her voice sounded false in its cheerful tone. Speaking or thinking of anything serious must be avoided. Not tonight. Not...now. Not ever. For it would break her heart into pieces.

Spence settled in and placed the tray between them. As he nibbled on a piece of cheese, she helped herself to the grapes.

"Phil, I've been thinking. You and I could...."

Oh, no.

She immediately stiffened; her breath caught in her throat. "Spence, you're a darling man. There is no 'you and I.' It's not possible." Phil kept her voice gentle though her insides lay in complete turmoil.

"You do not care for me." He folded his arms and frowned.

"That is not it at all. Think about it. You're the son of a duke, and I-I-I'm not able to move about or be part of your world."

"I am not out and about in society! Who would care?" Spence demanded.

Frustration caused her quick temper to flare. He was ruining this perfect night. Her hunger disappeared, and she tossed the half-eaten grapes on the plate. "Your family would care! I will repeat it—you're the son of a duke. A damned duke! It cannot happen; it will *not* happen." Phil's face flushed hot in annoyance.

"I am a nobody. Not the spare and certainly not the heir. I am the peculiar one, the eccentric lordling who is worth a jot only for what I inherited. Not handsome or charming and far too strange for the front parlors. What's more, I am glad of it. Perhaps I'm outlandish in my habits and life state, but I have feelings." He pounded his chest, laying his hand flat above his heart. His emotions were raw, and Phil's heart tightened.

"Feelings that run deep and wide like a calm river, and like a calm river, little seems to happen, change, or take effect on it. But if you were to measure the strength of those feelings, their force would be powerful indeed." His commanding voice ended with a whisper of sincerity, resonating straight from his soul.

What to say?

Her heart ached for him. Phil cared far more than she should or would admit aloud. Could he be merely caught up in new sensations with having sex for the first time? Entirely possible. Yet, he seemed to know his mind. Regardless of his compelling words, her frustration flared further.

"I understand what you're saying, and you are *not* a nobody. Let us not discuss this tonight," she said, waving her arm in dismissal.

"When will we discuss it, as you walk out the door?"

"In a couple of days, when Boyle arrives with the wagon, I will leave, Spence. I *must*." He opened his mouth to speak, but she laid two fingers against his lips. "No more talk of this. Let us enjoy the rest of the night and our remaining time."

Spence tossed the piece of chicken he'd been eating onto the tray. "Very well. I will not talk anymore of it—right now. However, consider this, then I will say no more: I believe we are well suited. When Boyle arrives, I can leave with him, acquire a carriage and horses, pack up the books, dogs, and anything else we wish, and head to Penhaven."

She closed her eyes, her heart contracting in pain. Why did he insist on this path? A fleeting vision of her and Spence living in domestic and connubial bliss fluttered through her mind. She shook it away. Merely a dream. A fragment of what can never be. And the sooner he realized it, the better for them both.

"Live at your estate? And what of my life in London? I run a business, and it is profitable enough. I'm independent, beholden to no one. Why would I give that up?" She popped a grape in her mouth, not daring to look at him. "Besides, you do not want a woman who has been with dozens of men. A woman so jaded she no longer feels anything. I am thirty-three years of age, Professor. Old by most standards of society. Older than *you*. You need a companion of a sweet temperament, an untouched young miss who will worship you. This conversation grows tedious. Do speak of another topic."

Before I shatter apart.

IF IT WERE PHYSICALLY possible for a heart to break in two, then Spencer experienced the sensation. Her words were spoken in a voice devoid of emotion; frost coated every word. He might be convinced of her indifference if he hadn't read the stark misery on her face. Her brows furrowed, her mouth twisted in sadness, yet her cheeks flushed crimson with infuriation.

One thing he'd learned these past days is that Phil did not hide her emotions as well as she thought. Deep down, she didn't believe the unkind words flung at him. He saw the proof in her tense expression.

How to persuade her she was everything he wanted, needed, and craved for?

He would never stymie her independence. Any money she made from her business would be hers alone. Hell, if she wanted to keep the business, that was fine with him as long as she hired someone else to run it, for he wanted her at his side—forever.

Selfish of him and also arrogant. Perhaps she didn't want him. No, what they shared earlier in this bed proved that theory wrong. No discussion? Fine. Spencer picked up the tray and laid it on the nearby table. Turning toward her, he leaned in and kissed her. He would show her what deep emotions she stirred in him.

Phil stiffened as if trying to steel herself from experiencing desire. He dove deeper, and his tongue tangled with hers. The kiss grew desperate, fierce, and passionate. With a soft moan, Phil returned it, proving at once that she wanted him as much as he yearned for her.

He unhooked the corset, and the garment fell away. All she wore were stockings. Magnificent breasts and creamy alabaster skin filled his vision. With a quick motion, Spencer slipped out of his trousers and threw them aside. Skin against skin, he longed for the sensation. Phil lay flat, and he rose above her, balancing on his arms. Phil grabbed an envelope from the nearby table. After slipping the sheath on his stiff prick, she explored his torso, her fingers trailing across his chest and down his stomach.

Spencer never liked anyone touching him; even with his family, he had to learn when to return a hug or shake someone's hand. But with Phil, he didn't have to think twice about how and when to respond. It came naturally as if he was born to make love to Phil.

Moving his hand between her legs, he teased her curls and closed his lips over her breast. She cried out as he plunged two fingers inside her.

Wet. Welcoming.

Bringing them both to the brink, Spencer removed his fingers and fumbled, trying to enter her. His skin grew hot with embarrassment, his inexperience rearing up once again. Grumbling, he cursed under his breath, his breathing uneven.

Phil kissed his cheek. "Calm, Spence. It's all right."

Her gently spoken words had the desired effect, and he exhaled. As always, she soothed his inner turmoil with her voice and a kiss.

She gripped his unruly shaft and guided him in.

Spencer sank deeper, then stilled.

He'd come home. This is where he was meant to be. Always.

To the end of his days.

Skin to skin, he reveled in the heat they generated. How her inner muscles clutched him in a possessive, intimate embrace. They fit together as a well-oiled machine with the proper working gears. This an exciting analogy considering he wished to pump her as hard and fast as a piston.

Although Spencer innately understood it would be best to go about this in a decidedly deliberate manner. Threading his fingers through hers, Spencer raised their clasped hands above their heads. He kissed her passionately while moving in and out of her with agonizing slowness.

Phil moaned, her back arching with each glide. Yes. *This.* He did it repeatedly, over and over, until both were covered in a thin sheen of perspiration. To hell with glancing at the clock, though he knew a good deal of time had passed. Controlling his release became difficult as he teetered on the edge of sensual oblivion. Phil neared her release, too. Her skin flushed, lips parted, and cries were husky and raw.

"What can I do? Tell me what to do," he rasped in her ear.

"Hook your arms behind my knees. Tilt me upward," she replied breathlessly. "Yes. There. Now, thrust hard and fast. I'm close."

The change in angle caused him to slip in deeper. Speeding up the pace also inflamed his arousal to unknown heights. Phil scored the skin on his back with her nails as she hooked her ankles across his arse.

Then, something infinitely magical happened. They both reached their peak simultaneously, clutching each other tightly and shuddering. Embracing, they lay for several minutes until their breathing regulated once again.

The clock on the mantel bonged twelve times. Midnight. As he hoped, he was inside her as the new year began. He kissed her long, deep, and with a poignancy that either of them could not deny.

Undeniably a happy new year. I cannot think of a better way to ring in the new.

If he had his way, he would ring in every new year for the rest of his life in just this fashion.

Together. Joined. Loving.

Spencer made one resolution. Before Phil departed, he would convince her they belonged together and that he yearned to share his life with her.

And he would tell her—that he loved her.

Chapter 16

NEW YEAR'S DAY TURNED out to be bright, the first time the sun had shone since Phil arrived at Spence's isolated hunting lodge. A fresh layer of snow blanketed the horizon; it sparked under the bright illumination. Hopefully, the sun would stay high in the sky long enough to melt enough snow, allowing Boyle and his wagon to arrive on schedule in about two days.

The sooner, the better.

Her defenses grew weaker each time she and Spence touched. Last night they fell asleep in each other arms once again. At two in the morning, she awoke and slipped into her room. Phil should be cloistered away, neither seeing nor speaking to him. Or touching or kissing or—making love. It would be the intelligent and sensible thing to do. But she couldn't stay away.

Could they become a couple?

Perhaps not in the conventional sense; however, she *could* be his mistress. Decide on a length of time and even fashion a contract since such arrangements were standard in the upper echelons of society. Phil would need to find someone to run the Starling Club for her. There was Darius; he had proven to be competent and trustworthy.

Why not carve out a little corner of happiness—for a year or two? Obviously, if he married, she would not continue as his mistress. The thought of him sharing his bed with another woman caused a roll of nausea to move through her.

Already staking a claim—a colossal mistake.

Phil had made a long-term plan for what remained of her life. At least five more years were needed to save the money required to live out the rest of her days in comfort. She could do so in a small part of England where no one knew her or her former occupation. She could negotiate a sum from Spence for her services as mistress and sell the brothel to make up the rest. With this plan, she could retire in two or three years instead of five.

A sound arrangement.

Phil would wait for him to mention it again, and if he didn't before she departed, she would stick with her original pact. In reality, it was all she could offer under the circumstances. There was no other reasonable option. A year or two with Spence would give her glorious memories to treasure in the lonely years to come, for she was not ready to say a permanent goodbye. Not yet. But wouldn't it hurt worse in two years' time? No doubt. But those beautiful reminiscences would sustain her. She hoped.

Phil clutched the dusty drapes as she stared out the window into nothingness. Her life was as empty as the horizon before her. But she had to admit that the small sloping hills had a stark beauty.

Yes, Empty.

Phil wanted to experience something...anything other than the predictable tedium of her life. She experienced plenty, including an overload of intense emotions and sensations that only made her confused, aggravated, and unsure. That is why she took this assignment, because of the utter emptiness of her life.

But because of this time with Spencer Hornsby, she never felt more alive.

As soon as Phil returned to civilization, she must send a telegraph informing her staff of her whereabouts. But would anyone care? The people at the club were not her family. They were not even her friends.

Regardless, Phil would not be collecting the rest of the fee for this "job," as it ceased being one after the first day. What she shared with

Spencer Hornsby could not be measured in pounds and shillings. This magnificent week would be forever etched in her memory, and she did not want it tainted by the exchange of further coin.

And yet she considered becoming his mistress. Somewhat hypocritical under the circumstances. Being his mistress would be a separate matter. Or was she deluding herself? Enough speculation, her head ached. And if Phil were to admit the truth, her heart also ached.

It was time to face the day. Dressed in her striped gown once again, she headed downstairs. The study door was ajar, and the temptation to explore Spence's domain was too great to disregard. After poking her head through the door, she quickly looked around. A fire crackled and snapped in the hearth, but no Spence or hounds. He must have taken them for a breath of air.

Phil paused momentarily to study the room, then strode to the bookcases and scanned the titles—books on philosophy and history, by the looks of it. Ancient and dusty, she observed, they must be from his grandfather's time.

Phil walked to one of the tables and unrolled one of the scrolls. A map. Her finger traced along the boundaries of certain countries. There was Constantinople. Spence had mentioned the ancient city during their fireside chat. Shoving aside a stack of papers to get a better look at the map, a fine powder arose to surround her.

God, the dust!

Coughing, she moved aside another pile of books knocking a few scrolls to the floor. After picking them up, Phil reached into her side pocket, pulled out a cloth, and started to clean the table, lifting more books and maps to reach underneath.

"What are you doing?" Spence boomed. The dogs barked in unison, causing her to jump and drop several maps. He snatched up the parchments, his face thunderous. "No one is to touch my work!" His voice was fierce, his manner cold and imperious. "Step away from the table at once! Do you understand? Get out!"

Phil sputtered, about to explain she was only dusting and hadn't disturbed...much. How dare he vent his spleen in such a matter? He marched toward her, his expression dark and dangerous, enough to cause her to reverse her steps.

His eyes glowed with an inner heat that had nothing to do with desire. "Get. Out."

With the cloth still clutched in her hand, Phil ran from the room and slammed the door behind her. The muffled sound of the dogs barking followed her all the way to the kitchen. Once there, she tossed the cloth aside and leaned against the counter, her chest heaving not only from her exertions but with fury.

Bizarre man!

To lose control like that because she *dared* to touch his belongings. His work. By his own admission, he described himself as strange. How right he'd been! Phil picked up an empty pot and flung it against the opposite wall.

Bastard!

The pan knocked loose a jagged chunk of plaster. She could only do one thing to calm the rage boiling in her veins.

Clean.

THE AFTERNOON PASSED by in a rush of activity. Phil didn't prepare breakfast or lunch, and, as far as she was concerned, the professor could starve. She waited for him to come to the kitchen to seek a meal, but he stayed clear.

Although she worried about Theodora and Justinian, they needed food. After quickly inspecting the root cellar, she noticed more of the leftover chicken was gone. The professor must have fed the dogs that morning before she arose. Perhaps he ate then as well.

Glancing down at her dress, she frowned. It was utterly ruined. She should have removed it. Stains covered the garment from the bodice to the mid-knee. Anger had clouded her mind most of the day, and she neglected to use the apron. However, she made quite a dent in the appearance of the kitchen.

During the rash cleaning spree, Phil had placed all the rubbish and broken crockery in large wooden crates, then scrubbed layers of grime off the counters and the sink basin. The working water pump enabled her to wash the dishes and pans that could be salvaged. Wiping away the perspiration from her forehead with her sleeve, she spied the tub sitting in the corner. A bath would be heavenly. She could try scrubbing the stains from her gown while at it.

First, she should haul the large crates outside. It was up to the peculiar professor what he decided to do with them. Once she opened the door, a cold blast of air hit her, temporarily seizing her breath. The sun was setting, and the warmth it provided was long gone. The temperature must have plunged rather swiftly as a heavy ice fog hung low across the horizon.

She dragged one of the heavy crates out the door with great effort. A loud rip of material filled her hearing. The seam had let go under her arm.

Bloody great.

Stepping back inside, she started as one of the dogs stood in the middle of the room cocking its head at her.

"Theodora, I presume? Come looking for a bite to eat?"

The dog snorted, wagged her tail, and swung its steady gaze toward the open door. With a burst of speed, the animal bolted past her outside into the heavy mist disappearing from sight.

Phil covered her mouth in shock. According to Spence, the dog was aged and not in the best of health. Yet, the beast moved quickly enough. What if the dog lost its way and perished? Spence would be heartbroken, and it would be all her fault. And she didn't want to hurt him any more than absolutely necessary.

Without further thought, Phil ran outside, calling Theodora's name. The sound traveled far in the cold twilight air, but there was no response. Venturing farther into the ice fog, her slippered feet numbed with the cold. She lifted her skirts to ease her path through the close-to-knee-high snow.

Damn the beast!

Phil turned in a circle scanning the horizon, but the snow had covered everything in a great blanket of white. Nothing was visible, not even the house. All turned around; she didn't know which way to travel. Blast her poor sense of direction. Blowing on her reddened knuckles, she tried desperately to warm them. She might as well head to the house and inform Spence that his dear pet had done a runner—yet another thing for him to be annoyed with her about.

Which direction *was* the place?

A gust of wind captured the loose snow and swirled it all around her, making visibility impossible, covering the path she had made with her footprints. How would she find her way back? She took a tentative step, then another. Phil squinted, trying to locate the light glowing from the kitchen to guide her. No luck. Perhaps she was headed in the wrong direction. A knot of queasiness settled deep inside her.

Doing an about-face and shivering from the wind and snow, she walked forward. The slippers made traversing difficult. Phil tottered precariously as it was an effort to stay upright. She should've worn her boots. Also shouldn't have bolted outdoors without a thought.

Happy bloody New Year.

Thus far, it turned out to be a disaster.

Taking another step, she skidded in the snow, landing on her side. A hot blade of pain shot through her ankle and rolled up her leg with lightning speed. Flexing her ankle, relief covered her at the realization that it wasn't broken. At worst, it might be sprained. After two attempts, she managed to stand upright.

Now what? Pick a direction.

Limping, she took several tentative steps and tumbled down an embankment.

I'm going to die in bloody Wales.

Chapter 17

THERE WERE NUMEROUS times during the day Spencer was tempted to seek Phil out and apologize profusely. His abhorrent burst of temper deserved an acknowledgment of contrition. Pride caused him to hesitate. And a profound embarrassment. He would be admitting to a weakness in his character, one he fought hard to conceal. All his life, he was called the duke's odd son. What happened with Phil became another random episode in many such disturbing incidents.

Everything in his life contained a specific order, much like his mind. His family and the servants understood they were to stay clear of his belongings. When someone laid their hands on his possessions, it often flew him into a rage.

As a rule, he was not a volatile man. His nature, on the whole, was calm and serene in most circumstances, almost to the point that his family and others wondered if he possessed anything as fundamental as human emotions. He had learned to hide them in those compartmentalized rooms of his mind.

Yet, he allowed Phil in his rooms.

Even more astonishing is that he allowed her to shave him and handle his toiletries. How he reveled in her touch, absorbing the gentle, caring way in which she'd groomed him. Amazingly, she didn't mock him about his various character quirks or sexual inexperience.

Spencer thought he had tackled the worst of his demons. Perhaps he found a woman he could allow within his solidly-drawn boundaries. A woman willing to live a sober life of solitude at a somewhat isolated estate. He would give his whole heart and undivided attention to such a woman. It would be a lot to ask of anyone.

But now this.

How to explain?

After all these years, he didn't understand it, and neither did his family. One incident at ten years of age had him curled up in his mother's lap, sobbing hysterically while his father paced and wrung his hands with worry. A doctor was called in. After the examination, he declared that Spencer should be placed in an asylum with shock treatments as a possible cure.

Thank God his father had immediately dismissed the doctor with a severe tongue lashing to send him on his way. Regardless, word spread of the "mad son of the duke," which caused Spencer to withdraw to his books and academia.

No one stood by him other than his family. Well, later at school, there were his few friends. His parents and brothers did their best to protect him and minimize the incidents. Regardless of their loving care, he experienced sporadic events through the years. Now he had exposed Phil to his inner demons. If she held any feelings for him at all, he might have just killed them.

Theodora, wet and shivering, loped into the room, barking furiously. He wondered where the dog had wandered off to. Justinian raised his head, looking between him and Theodora as if trying to ascertain the cause of the alarm. Theodora was not a dog given to histrionics. Something was up.

Spencer jumped to his feet. "What is it, old girl?"

Still barking, the dog faced the doorway and stepped into the hall. Facing him, her growls and woofs became insistent. Justinian, no doubt as confused as Spencer, fell into step behind him. They followed Theodora down the stairs and into the kitchen. The door was open, with snow blowing in through the entrance. The cold wind could slice a man in two.

Phil. Where is she?

Theodora woofed gruffly to gain his attention, then bolted through the door into the darkening twilight.

"Justinian, sit. Stay."

The dog obeyed him immediately. Spencer's heart lurched in his chest. He knew his canine companion well. Theodora would not raise such an alarm unless there were an urgent need. Visibility was poor. Blowing snow and a thick, frosty mist made it difficult to move about. Good thing he knew the grounds. Bile rose in his throat, burning hot with fear, as he chased after Theodora's frantic barks toward the edge of the cliff.

Dear God, no.

Peering over the precipice, he frantically searched, but the layer of white interspersed with the increasing darkness blanked his vision. Damn, he should return to the house, light a lantern... At that moment, as if by providence, the mist dissipated enough for him to make out part of a figure half-buried in the snow and lying precariously on the ledge.

"Phil! Philomena!" he cried.

No reply.

Theodora barked, and Spencer patted her head. "Good job, old girl. Well done."

The ledge, though narrow, was less than ten feet down from the end of the ridge. He could descend quickly enough if he were careful. But then they would both be stuck. No, he was tall enough that he could manage to clamber back even with Phil over his shoulder if needs must. The rock face was not smooth but contained jagged edges for possible climbing: no time to lose or ascertain the location of a lantern and rope. The temperature grew colder by the minute.

Besides, if she gained consciousness and rolled the wrong way, she would fall over the edge and perish. Spencer grasped the border of the cliff and lowered himself. His booted foot found a rock jutting, then another until he was perched precariously on the outcrop. A blast of cold snow hit his face, the flakes settling on his lashes. The bitter wind howled all around them.

"Phil!"

She lay still, not responding. A palpable fear took hold, chilling him more deeply than the bitter wind. Spencer brushed away the snow from her face and gently tapped her cheeks. Phil moaned and stirred but did not open her eyes. He wasn't sure where he found the strength, but he crouched down and slid her limp form over his shoulder. Taking a deep breath, he exhaled while shifting her weight into a more comfortable position. He glanced up. Theodora peered over the edge and woofed.

"Yes, old girl. I'll be careful."

Spencer remained focused on the task and, with deliberate and measured movements, climbed the rock face until he could slide Phil gently off his shoulder onto the ground above. He lifted himself upward, then scooped her up into his arms. Every muscle in his body screamed in protest at the exertion.

With Theodora leading the way, he returned to the house without further incident. Justinian gave him a welcoming woof. As he stepped into the kitchen, the most terrible feeling overcame him. Spencer could not bear it if anything happened to Phil. Shaking from the cold but also from raw terror, he had never experienced such a wave of despair and a sense of loss before. In that instant, he knew he would give up his life to save hers.

Chapter 18

THE FIRST SENSATION Phil experienced was bone-chilling shivers like she was coated in frost. Slowly, she opened her blurry eyes. Flickering flames caught her attention, and she realized she was staring at a fire in the hearth. She lay before it—where? A gentle woof caught her attention. She was in the study. Theodora and Justinian stared down at her.

"Thank God, Phil. You're awake. You had us all quite worried."

Spence.

He kneeled next to her. Fast-melting snow was evident on his clothes and in his tousled hair. The look of concern also showed relief and tenderness.

Phil tried to speak, but all that came out was a dry croak. Spence wrapped a warm quilt around her as he'd done with Theodora days before. Pulling her close, he rubbed the cloth against her goose-bumped skin, whispering words of reassurance.

Phil could not hold back the tears. The stark fact hit her then and there as he held her: she loved him. Against all her logical instinct and reasoning, she had fallen in love with this man. Over the past several days, her feelings intensified exponentially, and she tried to ignore the sensation, but at this moment, holding her, consoling her with no regard for his own comfort, removed the last of her denial.

She was deeply and irretrievably in love with Lord Spencer Hornsby.

The admission made her cry harder, for there could never be anything lasting between them. Not ever.

"There, don't cry, Phil. You're safe."

No, she wasn't safe. She was in absolute peril—especially her vulnerable heart.

"We should get you out of these wet clothes immediately. You've lost your shoes." His soft baritone caused her heart to ache with longing.

Oh, she was utterly lost.

He lifted her foot and gently rubbed feeling back into it, then did the same with the other. She flinched and groaned as Spence felt around her ankle.

"Does it hurt? I do not feel any broken bones."

"A little. Maybe a sprain," she answered, her voice hoarse.

Reaching under her gown, he removed her stockings and laid them before the fire. Together, they pulled off the rest of her damp garments. The brush of his fingers against her skin ignited a flame deep within, warming her more than any blanket. He wrapped the quilt around her tighter, murmuring words of comfort.

"W-W-What about you? You are...are soaking wet." Phil shivered, her teeth chattering.

Spence stood. "I have clothes we can wear, plus I have a flask of brandy in my room. Will you be all right for a moment? I'll return swiftly, I promise."

She nodded as she pulled the quilt closer.

Sitting to her left, Justinian laid his head on her lap, staring at her with an adoring look that made the tears fall faster. Theodora lay opposite.

Spence nodded. "That's it, lad, watch over Phil. Good job, old girl. Warm yourself by the fire. Theodora is the heroine here; she led me straight to you."

"Oh, Spence." She sniffled and wiped her eyes with the corner of the quilt.

It had been decades since she allowed tears to fall like this. Spence kissed her forehead, lightly wiping the remaining tears away from her cheeks. He departed. His rapid footfalls echoed in the room. Phil poked her hands out from under the quilt and patted both dogs.

"My dear friends," she whispered.

Justinian whimpered and leaned into her touch. The warm quilt helped elevate the chill from her bones, but still, she shivered. How frightening to fall off a cliff. And clumsy.

My God, she could have perished.

The thought caused a ripple of fright to knot her insides, mixing with the turbulent emotions already there. Phil had no clue how to make sense of any of them.

Spence returned in a matter of moments. He quickly stripped off and laid his wet clothes beside hers. Regardless of her weakened and chilled state, hot desire rushed through her as she admired his lean musculature. Leaning down, he handed her a nightshirt and slipped one over his head as he sat beside her.

Since her shaking made it difficult to poke her arms through the sleeves, Spence assisted her. Again, his gentle touch calmed her. Emanating from his garment was the sensual scent of spice and a masculine essence that belonged solely to him. Spence hung a large towel above the fire.

He handed her a silver flask. "Brandy. Take a deep gulp. It will warm you." Since her hand trembled, he clasped his over hers to keep it steady and raised the flask to her lips. "Drink, go on."

The liquid burned a fiery trail down her throat. It helped dissipate the chill. Spence tipped the flask to his lips and drank. He returned it to her, reached for the towel, and laid it across Theodora.

"She came into my study barking quite furiously, then led me straight to you. I shudder to think how long you could have lain there exposed to the elements. My damned pride kept me from seeking you out to apologize for my abhorrent behavior." She started to speak, but Spence raised his hand to silence her.

"It's hard to explain one's demons. I have had these—episodes—since childhood. Back then, they would manifest as crying jags, enough to worry my parents and prompt them to call a medical professional. Later, as I grew older, the crying turned to rages. It does not happen often, and I apologize that you were exposed to my weakness of character." Spence continued stroking the warm cloth on Theodora, who sighed and curled closer. The dog closed her eyes and fell asleep.

"Don't call it a weakness. Y-y-you simply do not like anyone handling your belongings. I knew better."

"Yet, I permitted you to enter my room and shave me. I did not vent my spleen then. There is no rhyme or reason for my reactions. Perhaps my father should have placed me in the asylum at the doctor's suggestion. Perhaps shock treatments might have helped."

Phil snuggled next to Spence, laying her head on his shoulder. "Your father was quite right not to allow such barbaric treatment. You're *not* mad. I should have realized and not reacted with such fury. I should have understood and helped you. We are not perfect, Spence. No one is. We all have demons of one sort or another."

"I do not deserve your compassion. What were you doing outside?"

Phil took another small sip of brandy and handed the flask to Spence. "When I'm angry, I clean. The door was open because I dragged crates of rubbish outside. Theodora came into the kitchen and bolted out the door. You mentioned earlier that she's old and not entirely well. I didn't think. I ran after her and lost my bearings."

She sighed and burrowed closer to Spence, reveling in his scent and warmth. "What if she got lost, you would have been devastated. I had to find her. I slipped and fell, hit my head, and wrenched my ankle for good measure."

Spence sat the flask on the floor, then tunneled his hands through her wet hair. "There is a small bump. Do you feel dizzy or faint?"

The concern in his voice touched her. "No, but I do feel foolish. Leave it to me to fall off a cliff."

"Thank God a ledge hampered you from falling farther. When I think about what could have happened to you." He tilted her chin upward and gave her a tender kiss, then a brilliant smile. "Once in a while, Theodora has a burst of energy and goes for a sprint. She always returns."

"I didn't know that. I thought she had run away. Now I feel even more stupid."

"I lit the fire in my room. I'll take you up and tuck you into bed."

"Can we stay here a bit longer? I'm warming up surrounded by you and the dogs."

The cozy intimacy comforted her. It was as if they were all a family. The sentimental thought caused a lump of emotion to form in her throat. Having a near-death experience was causing havoc with her feelings, fueling a yearning for a life she had never contemplated.

Her and Spence—and the wolfhounds? Happily ever after?

It was not possible.

"If you wish," he said.

"I do. Hold me closer."

He did, tucking her head under his chin. "I haven't eaten today."

"Nor have I. Quite the New Year's Day."

Phil started to drift off to sleep. The last she remembered, she was being carried upstairs.

FOR TWO HOURS, SPENCER sat by the bed and watched Phil sleep. He wouldn't leave her side. When they were downstairs, he nearly declared his deep and abiding love for her, but it was not the right moment.

The sun had set, and the only light came from the illumination from the fire and a lit candelabrum on the mantel. A warm amber glow filled the room with shadow and light, dancing as if in an ethereal waltz. How innocent and sweet she looked in this radiance.

May he never experience such a crushing sense of despondency ever again. But wouldn't he relive it when she departed in two days?

The accident drove the salient point home that staying in this remote place was foolhardy. He could not keep her here against her will, short of locking her in a room. Spencer would have to convince her by other means. His grandfather only used the manor a few weeks a year, not for months on end. It was time to stop hiding away and embrace life—at least as much as he could.

Long ago, Spencer gave up hope of finding anyone to love him. His many eccentric ways would send any sane woman running in the opposite direction— or man, for that matter. At university, a young man had shown an interest in him, and, for the briefest of moments, Spencer considered exploring the attraction. Desperate to experience anything, he tried to talk himself into feeling something toward the youth, but he did not. The friendship ended awkwardly, with Spencer all the more convinced he would not be able to handle amorous relationships with either gender.

Here lay the one person who touched his heart.

She cared for him, or why else would she tear outside into the fog and blowing snow to find his dog? With her gentle guidance and tender touch, she brought out everything he desperately tried to hide. The capacity to love and to feel desire existed within him, and Phil proved it.

The fact that she risked her life so he wouldn't be devastated if anything happened to Theodora spoke more than mere words could describe. But in these past days, he learned Phil could be stubborn and resolute. How to convince her to accept him, flaws and all?

Phil stirred and moaned. Spencer sat on the edge of the bed and laid his hand on her forehead. A little warm. It would be prudent to monitor her for the next several hours.

"What's the time?" she asked.

"The hour is near seven. I'll bring us food. We shall have a picnic here on the bed. Not quite sure I can manage tea, but I will endeavor to try." He trailed the back of his fingers across her pale cheeks. "Rest, Phil. You do not want to catch a chill or develop a fever. I suggest you stay abed for the rest of the night and most of tomorrow. And I will stay here with you."

"What of your research?" she asked.

"You are more important to me. I will see you well. We have much to discuss, but not tonight. Stay under the covers." He tucked the hem of the bedspread under her chin, kissed her forehead and cheeks, then gave her a gentle but lingering kiss on her trembling lips.

As he descended the stairs, he wondered how on earth he could convince her of his love and devotion.

And to stay with him.

For always.

Chapter 19

PHIL WAS MORTIFIED to use a chamber pot, but Spence refused to carry her outside to the necessary, claiming she could catch a further chill. He wasn't wrong, as she battled a slight fever through the night, one moment cold and shivering and the next kicking off the blankets and perspiring. Spence stayed by her side, held her close when she needed warmth and comfort, and administered cold water when her parched lips asked for it.

Surprisingly, she even caught a few hours of sleep but nothing of any substance. She was not used to having someone watch over her and protect her like this. Phil found that she had reveled it.

With the rise of the morning sun came fresh worries: Spence and what he wished to discuss remained at the forefront of her mind. She loved him, and because of that, she should leave him in peace and not allow sentiment to enter the discussion. They had known each other for only a few days; the situation was preposterous. They could not be together, not in the long term. It wasn't feasible.

The fleeting notion of becoming his mistress *should* also be off the table. Phil wanted to spare her battered heart. Loving him as she did, and entering into a carnal agreement, would prolong the agony.

No, best to cut it clean.

Quite the change from what she was contemplating yesterday. People recovered and mended from broken hearts, did they not? In the meantime, she would gather all the memories she could as this week with Spence would have to sustain her well into her dotage.

Phil sat upright, stuck her leg out from under the blankets, and flexed her ankle. Though badly bruised, she was able to move it. It was not sprained then—all the better.

Spence entered the room carrying a tray. "I managed to light the stove properly this time. The water boiled, and I prepared hot tea. Unfortunately, I didn't have as much luck with the toast. There is fruit and cheese...again."

She smiled. "I'm feeling much better thanks to your ministrations. By suppertime, I'll be able to cook us a meal. As for toast, I'll make us some tonight in front of the fire. I do an excellent fireplace toast and cheese."

Spence sat next to her and laid the tray between them. She picked up the mug of tea and sipped.

"Is it adequate?" he asked.

"Well, it's better than last night's, I'll say that much."

Spence laughed, a low sensual rumble that sparked her arousal. Of course, he didn't have to do much to heighten her desire.

"The dogs will be grateful about dinner. They are tired of bread and cheese as well. I gave them the last chicken this morning, which should hold them over." He lifted his mug and sipped, then grimaced. "I imagine that this tastes very similar to warm dishwater. It will have to do. May I ask you a question? About your life?"

"All right," she replied hesitatingly, unsure of what he would ask.

"Tell me about your brothel and the people there. Do you like them?"

"My employees? Yes, I do. We are not all close friends as such, but comrades in arms. Trying to survive our circumstances. We protect each other." Phil pulled the blanket about her shoulders. "Everyone working for me was in dire straits when I hired them. I have one man in my employ, Darius Brownlow. I found him beaten in an alley. He was a boxer who crossed the wrong sort. They had left him for dead. He acts as a bodyguard and assists me in running the place. Why do you ask?"

"I wanted to know if there are people in your sphere that you care about and that there are people who care about you. Though not strictly a family, I am glad you have support."

"And you have such backing from your family?" Phil asked, her voice soft.

Spence nodded. "We all love each other."

"I'm curious why your caring and loving family allowed you to go off alone to such a remote place?" She clasped his arm briefly. "I'm not saying you aren't capable, far from it."

"I understand what you mean. They did voice their concern, but I insisted. I wanted to prove to them that I could manage. Accomplish something worthwhile. Perhaps I needed to prove it to myself most of all. I want to be considered for more than my—affliction. I wanted to see if I could function." Spence sighed as he placed his teacup on the tray.

"I am not certain I will be able to teach, despite my brave plans," he continued. "But I want to attempt a few lectures. Stand on my own two feet. Be what is considered—normal. I'm not, you know."

Phil laced her fingers through his. "What *is* normal? What society dictates? Bugger that. I like you just the way you are. Don't ever change."

He kissed her hand, then nuzzled his cheek against it. "My dear Phil."

The emotion was becoming too much once again. Best to change the subject.

"What have you planned for today?" she inquired, giving him a tremulous smile.

"After this rather pitiable breakfast, I thought I would read to you for a while. Then I will pour you a hot bath. Take the rest of the afternoon to relax until dinner if you wish. Or am I being presumptive in arranging your day?"

Read? That glorious voice?

How will she be able to bear it?

Phil shook her head to clear away the sensual images. "Not at all. I am basking in your attention. I'm not used to such consideration from a man."

"Allow me to say this, Phil. I have deep feelings for you. I've not reached the age of thirty without knowing my own mind, and I am quite capable of discerning the difference between sex and lovemaking. I would have never agreed to physical relations unless salient emotions were at the core. It's why I remained a virgin. It would never be a casual dalliance for me. I haven't developed these feelings for you because you're my first lover. They were there before I joined with you."

Spence pulled his hand from hers and met her gaze full-on. "I wanted you to know it's not a green lad's infatuation. Nor have I found a new object to obsess over. It is real, deep, and very poignantly felt."

Oh, bloody hell.

How to answer such a declaration?

He all but said that he loved her, though he was approaching this cautiously, revealing his feelings by degrees. Every instinct in her wished to hold him tight, sob into his chest that she loved him more than her own life—such as it was.

Honestly, she *had* believed his feelings for her existed because she'd been his first. At least a little bit. Apparently not. A cold stab of fright clutched her. If he loved her as much as she loved him, this parting would devastate them both. It would be utterly ruinous and heartbreaking.

"I'm not sure what to say—"

"Say nothing. Think over my words. We'll discuss this later." He stood. "I'll wash up, take the dogs for a stroll, and return to read to you. Enjoy the dishwater tea." Spence gave her a brief smile and disappeared into his dressing room.

A dull ache throbbed between her eyes. This was all too much. More transpired in the past several days than in the previous fifteen years. She needed time to sort through it all. Oh, why couldn't this have been a simple, meaningless rut? A job and nothing more?

Instead—it meant *everything.*

"LIKE SOULS THAT BALANCE joy and pain, with tears and smiles from heaven again. The maiden Spring upon the plain. Cause in a sunlit fall of rain."

Spence sat by the bed. His deep, dulcet tone rolled seductively over Tennyson's *Sir Launcelot and Queen Guinevere.* Every roll of syllables set her heart to drumming.

"A man has given all other bliss and all his worldly worth for this. To waste his whole heart in one kiss. Upon her perfect lips."

Spence placed the book on the bed. Framing her face, he gave her such a heartrending look that she hovered close to tears. The gentle kiss contained a fiery heat, though it was all too brief for her liking.

"You read very well," Phil said, her voice quivering with emotion.

"I deliberately chose this poem. I meant every word." Spence tossed aside the covers and lifted her into his arms, causing her to squeal. "Your bath awaits, Queen Guinevere. It must be at a proper temperature by now."

"You don't have to carry me," she laughed.

"I like having you in my arms." Spence smoothly descended the stairs as if carrying her was no hardship.

Once inside the kitchen, he lowered her slowly, her body rubbing against his as she tried to find the floor with her bare toes.

He means every word of the poem.

Phil's heart swelled with love. He kissed her again. Then with a swift motion, he pulled off the nightshirt.

"You're entirely beautiful. A veritable Venus." He laid a hot kiss on her shoulder. Lifting her once again, he gently set her in the tub. The temperature of the water held a rolling warmth that soothed as well as comforted.

Spence pulled over a chair and sat next to the tub. "I found your soap. Whenever I smell lavender, I will think of you." He moved the warm cloth across her body in long, sensual strokes. "If only this tub were bigger, I would join you," he whispered hotly in her ear.

She closed her eyes, and a moan slipped from her parted lips. He seduced not only with his voice but his words and touch. Considering he had no experience, he inherently understood how to tantalize her. The cloth moved across her breasts, hardening the nipples and causing heat to bloom deep inside.

After rinsing her hair, he assisted her out of the tub, then dried her. Phil's body tingled all over from his touch. He passed her a dressing gown. No doubt his as the hem of the garment scraped the floor as she tied it about her waist.

"You're spoiling me."

"Yes, I am. I quite enjoy it. What's next? A nap? Another cup of tepid tea?"

"I think a nap. I'm very relaxed. And you don't have to carry me. See?" She walked across the floor. "As long as I don't place much weight on it, it's fine. Wake me around half past four." She stepped closer. "And Spence?" She stood before him, brushing her breasts across his chest until he moaned. "Tonight, I will have a surprise for *you*."

"The toast and cheese?" he replied.

She laughed. "No, after. Something quite delicious." She brushed her fingers teasingly across the fall of his trousers, pleased to feel the hardness there. With a dazzling smile, she turned and hobbled from the room.

As Phil walked away, her smile disappeared. No matter what occurred between them —the poignant words and touches —she remained determined to leave.

It was the only sane and rational thing to do.

Chapter 20

THE SUPPER CONSISTED of a simple repast of ham, eggs, and fried potatoes. While it certainly filled Spencer, he hungered for much more.

Having her in his life felt real and natural. They had slipped into a seamless domestic rhythm he loathed to break. As tempted as he'd been to bring her to full arousal while in the tub, he held himself in check by giving her teasing, feather-like caresses enough to spark her desire but not inflame it.

Essentially, he laid the foundation for declaring his love and asking her to stay. You would think he would be used to rejection, but this particular refutation he dreaded most of all. He would be laying his heart and soul bare; however, he would regret it for the rest of his life if he did not.

They sat before the fireplace in his study, surrounded by blankets, pillows, and the two dogs. Phil speared a piece of bread at the end of the fireplace poker and held it over the flames. The cheese sizzled and bubbled as the bread toasted to a golden hue.

"I used to make this for my father. The last time was shortly before he died. We would sit before the fireplace, just the two of us, and he would tell me about his day. He was a doctor at St. Thomas's Hospital and always had a funny tale to tell. Or a gruesome one." A small smile curved about her lips at the recollection.

"How did your parents die?"

Phil inspected the bread and, seeing it required more toasting, shoved it above the flames. "The way most parents die together, in a senseless accident. Their carriage was traveling far too fast, and they were in a horrific collision with another. One minute they were here, and the next, gone—leaving me all alone. I wandered about our house in a state of shock. My aunt and uncle swooped in. The house was closed up, and the contents sold." She paused and frowned.

Spencer did not interrupt, nor did he encourage her to reveal more. He would hazard to guess that she rarely spoke of her past. The recollections were painful; it was plain to see.

After a few moments, she exhaled and continued. "My father held a responsible post. He made a good wage and was respected in the medical field. The money he set aside was passed to my aunt and uncle for my upkeep. Two years later, I was abducted from the train station and certainly did not see any benefits of that money." Phil paused, then shook her head.

"That sounds entirely selfish. But when I last visited them, I noticed the new furnishings. The money was spent; it wasn't even worth asking for. I wonder now if they even reported me missing or hired anyone to look for me. I doubt it." Phil scoffed. "They claimed that they did, and the fact I'm still dubious shows how bitter and cynical I've become." Her lips pulled into a thin line as she removed the bread from the flames. "We'll let it cool for a moment."

Potent fury clutched him tight. How dare her aunt and uncle treat her with such disdain and indifference? They should have greeted Phil with open arms, relieved and grateful she'd survived her ordeal. Instead, they judged her. They turned their backs on her.

What further fueled his ire? The overwhelming temptation to head to Cheapside, flush out this disgraceful couple, and toss them to the cobbles. Let them experience what it felt like to have no one to turn to and no means by which to live.

Spencer tried to mask his anger, but his voice shook with emotion nonetheless. "I am sorry. No child should lose a parent, let alone both at once. It must have been unbearable for you. You are the most courageous woman I have ever met. Give me their address. I will see justice done. I will tie them up in litigation and see them bankrupt. There are legal means available to pursue your inheritance." Never had such a surge of revenge overtaken him before.

"Oh, give over. I am a survivor; I'll grant you that. Be damned if I will be a victim. I took my fate into my own hands as there was no other family to turn to." Phil handed the toast to him, then commenced making her own. "I learned early on you have to look out for yourself as no one else will. As for justice, it doesn't matter. The money is gone. Taking them to court would only bring my past to light. They would use it against me. I don't need the drama. I've moved on."

"Yes, I see your point. Still, I would like nothing more than to give your uncle a thrashing. And your aunt a proper tongue lashing."

"I appreciate that, I do. But I can take care of myself."

"Yes, you can. Rather a lonely existence, is it not?" He bit into the toasted bread, relishing the explosion of hot cheese.

"I've accepted my lot in life. A lonely existence is also your chosen path. Look where you're staying. The life you've chosen."

"Yes, I prefer to be alone in most circumstances, but not all. Everyone yearns to be loved, Phil—even the most hardened and determined hermit. I do enjoy the company of my family in small doses, I grant you, but nevertheless, I love them dearly. I also have a few friends like the ones who hired you. I suppose they were well-meaning. At first, I resented their interference. Now I will thank them with all my heart for bringing you to me, even if it is for only a short duration."

"You know it must be." Phil sighed, biting into her toast.

"I know nothing of the sort. You're the one who refuses to discuss what is between us—or the possibility that there could be more."

Spencer popped the last bit of toast in his mouth and chewed, trying to keep his annoyance from rising to the surface.

Phil lifted her chin in stubborn defiance. "The discussion will turn into an argument; I can guarantee it. I'm putting it off as long as I can. Why not enjoy these last days together? I do not wish it to degenerate into accusations and hurt feelings. Besides, I've been through entirely too much the last twenty-four hours. Let us take this evening to relax and enjoy each other."

Spencer stared into the flames, his heart sinking. "You intend to reject me no matter what I have to say?"

Phil ate more of her toast, not answering. He waited, trying desperately to remain patient. Spencer watched her expression change from frustration to annoyance, then to puzzlement.

"I don't know," she replied, her voice soft.

"Well, at least you did not rebuff me outright. I will bend to your will for tonight, but hear me, Philomena McGrattan. Tomorrow night may be the last one, and we will discuss this at length. Do you agree?"

She met his gaze, and a slight frown curved about her mouth. "You're determined we will have this out. Fine. Tomorrow night. Are you ready for more toast and cheese?"

"Excellent change of topic. Well done. Not at this moment. What I do want is this surprise you mentioned." He gave her a playful wink, and it lightened her mood immediately. The furrow between her brows disappeared. Good, for he didn't wish to dwell on any negativity.

"I have not done this in years. I will no doubt make a hash of it." She rose up on her knees, clasped his shoulders, and pushed him down until he lay flat on the pillows and blankets. "Oral sex. My lips on your cock. Sucking and licking and taking you deep until you come."

Lord almighty.

Spencer hardened immediately at her erotic words. Pulling her down on top of him, he claimed her mouth, taking utter possession. The kiss spoke of everything he felt, passion, love, and a desire so intense he thought he would ignite into flames from the force of it. As they kissed, she unbuttoned his shirt, exposing his chest. Deftly moving her hand to the fall of his trousers, she pulled out his erect prick.

The kiss ended, and Phil slid down along his torso, leaned in, and closed her mouth over the swollen head of his shaft. The immediate wet warmth that encased him caused the breath to seize in his throat. His heart thumped at a rapid pace. When he finally exhaled, he couldn't stop the words from tumbling from his throat.

"Yes. God, yes. Take me deep." His voice contained a strange mix of a harsh command and a passionate pleading.

After a few tentative licks, Phil grasped him tight, squeezing as she soon found a rhythm. Taking him deep, she hollowed her cheeks, creating a suction that had his hips lifting off the floor with ecstasy.

Clutching the blanket tight with one hand, his groans filled the air. He grabbed a fistful of her silken hair with his free hand, twined it around his wrist, and gently encouraged her to take him deeper. The dogs acted unconcerned and continued to nap.

Spencer was wholly lost in a haze of ecstasy. Floating—that was the sensation. As if suspended in the clouds. Perhaps madness lay at his core. The exquisite pressure built. So close. Spencer cried out as he came. His head spun; his breathing ragged.

Phil smiled as she rose up on her knees.

"My. You are quite wild, Professor." She leaned in and kissed him. Her sweetness mixed with his musky taste. Intriguing. Lying next to him, she rested a hand on his heaving chest. "I may tease, but I enjoy how you hold nothing back. I quite admire you for it."

He exhaled, catching his breath at last. "Only with you, Philomena. Only you."

AS MUCH AS SHE ENJOYED and admired his unfettered responses and tender glances, they also concerned her. Phil trailed the tips of her fingers across his amazing cheekbones. He leaned into her touch, giving a husky moan in response. His whiskers scratched at her hand. Spence needed a shave. Perhaps she would give him one tomorrow.

No one should feel this much in such a short acquaintance, and she meant both of them. Though they hinted at the depth of emotions, they had not discussed them in detail. Unfortunately, he would insist they do so tomorrow night.

Phil could deny how she truly felt and be cruel and dismissive. Claim their assignation had merely been a paid assignment and nothing more. But she could not break his heart. How to convince him that a connection between them would be ruinous for him?

She must think of his future. Protect him from further censure and ridicule. The only way to achieve that goal would be to leave him, even though the prospect already had her heart and soul in tatters, but what else could she do?

Spence opened his eyes. The stunningly beautiful shade of blue always caught her breath. They shone with intelligence and affection. Her heart hitched in her chest. She had removed oral sex from her prossie repertoire long ago, never fond of it. With Spence? She thoroughly enjoyed it. Phil stifled a yawn, covering her mouth with her hand.

Spence kissed her cheek. "You're tired. We should head to bed."

She nodded, giving him a wan smile. Spence stood and lifted her with a sweep of his arms, then carried her to his bedroom. How she could get used to such attention. She curled her arms about his neck and laid her head against his chest, inhaling his spicy essence.

Phil swallowed back the tightness in her throat. Love was a foreign concept to her outside of what she felt for her late parents. Long ago, she vowed not to allow such complications into her life. To find it here, in a crumbling hunting lodge leaning precariously on the edge of a cliff in an inaccessible section of Wales—made no sense whatsoever.

Who would have thought the eccentric third son of a duke would be everything she yearned for?

She loved him.

And, after endless vacillating, including considering being his mistress, she concluded that she *must* leave him. To protect him from her past in order to save his reputation and standing.

The sadness flooding her soul would stay with her for the rest of her life.

Chapter 21

"TIME TO AWAKEN, MY dearest Phil." As Spence placed gentle, affectionate kisses on her cheek, he rolled his hips, making sure she could *not* possibly miss the hardness of his erection brushing against her arse.

"Do you have one of those sheaths nearby?" he whispered. "I may need your assistance."

Barely awake, and already he was aroused. My, how she could get used to this every morning. But she couldn't. Instead, Phil would continue to gather these sweet memories and treasure them. Phil retrieved an envelope from the cloth bag on the nearby table. Spence watched, his gaze intense, as she slid the condom on. She swiftly lifted the nightshirt over her head and tossed it aside.

"Lay back in the position you were before," he commanded.

My. The more experience he gained, the more he assumed the dominant role. She didn't mind. Not in the least. Spence turned out to be a passionate and lustful man. A remarkable discovery and almost as incredible as discovering it existed within herself.

He laid her leg on his thigh. "You're wet for me. I do not even have to check, do I, Phil?"

"No, you don't."

He entered her with a swift glide. While nibbling on her earlobe, he moved in and out of her with agonizing slow thrusts. They both writhed and moaned, prompting him to increase the pace. This position was entirely magnificent. Their bodies entwined, with him behind. She pushed back, taking him deeper.

Faster, they moved until her release caused her to cry out, the sound hoarse. A few minutes later, Spence groaned, softly saying her name repeatedly. He pulled her closer and nuzzled her neck. The whispered words of desire awakened her arousal again. He was still inside her as if he loathed breaking the connection. She understood it, for she longed to stay joined.

After several minutes, he kissed her cheek and rolled upright. The loss of his warmth caused her to shiver. "Breakfast?" he asked.

"Worked up an appetite, have you, Professor?" she teased.

Spence grinned. "Of course. So have you, I've no doubt. Are you feeling better?"

"Yes. Entirely recovered. You're a skilled healer, talented indeed."

He reached for his trousers and slipped them on. "Good. The sun is shining. Time to get the day underway."

"Is that an order?" Phil laughed.

"Well, let's call it a request." He tossed her the nightshirt and laughed when it hit her square in the face.

Later, they shared a hearty breakfast. After wiping his mouth on the napkin, Spence stood. "Join me in my study at two o'clock, will you?" He gave her a formal bow and a sly grin, then strode from the room.

What is he up to?

SPENCER FOUND IT HARD to concentrate on his research these past few hours. Instead, he packed up several of his maps and books. Regardless of the outcome of their discussion later tonight, he decided he would not be staying here at the manor.

If Phil stubbornly insisted on leaving him, he could not bear to reside here without her. She would haunt every cobwebbed crevice. Her husky voice and passionate moans would echo in the musty hallways of this manor and his mind. His heart and soul. Her scent would permeate and sear his senses, driving him insane with heartbreak and loss.

Leave it to him to drown in maudlin thoughts. He would not concede defeat as yet. There remained a little time to show her they were a perfect fit—and not only physically. He pulled back the draperies and gazed across the barren property. The sun made the snow glitter with the twinkle of a thousand diamonds; much had melted in the last twenty-four hours. With the road more passable, no doubt Boyle would arrive in the morning.

He could not ride in the wagon with her if she rejected his suggestion. How awkward. He could pay Boyle a king's ransom to return for him in the afternoon. The trip took over an hour and a half, though it probably would take longer because of the snow. He would purchase a large horse and carriage to accompany his prized possessions and friends—his books and dogs.

Penhaven would be an excellent place to recover from his broken heart. Overwhelming emotions caused a knot to form in his throat. Years ago, he retreated within his own world to avoid being hurt.

No one outside his family ever reached the most vulnerable part of him—his heart. But Philomena did in no time at all. Though he hid his emotions for years, the stark truth lay before him: he felt far too much. He loved Phil with a savage fierceness that was damned startling in its depth. He would be utterly devastated and shattered at her departure—a broken man.

What if she agreed to stay with him?

His heart leaped with joy at the possibility. He could go to the village with Boyle and, with purchased transportation, return to the manor. Phil would wait at the front entrance with Theodora and

Justinian standing at either side of her. God, how he longed for such a scenario. Someone to greet him. To share his quiet life. To love him unconditionally.

With a shaky sigh, Spencer stepped away from the window. He was a romantic fool. Apparently, he loved Phil far more than his books, antiquities, and wolfhounds, or this place, for that matter. Yes, a shocking discovery indeed.

A soft knock sounded at the door, and Phil slipped in, carrying a basin and a bundle of towels. "I know it's not two o'clock yet, but I thought you would like a shave."

Justinian woofed gently in greeting at her arrival. Phil cooed a greeting in return. His dog was entirely besotted with her, and he could not blame him. Today she wore the beautiful gold New Year's Eve gown and a large white apron to protect the fancy garment.

Phil motioned to the chair. He sat obediently as she wrapped a small towel about his neck. "Do you mind if I move a few of these books off the desk for the basin and implements?"

His insides clenched at the request, but he fought the urge to react negatively. Spencer must show control in these situations, especially if the possibility of a future together becomes a reality.

Swallowing back his anxiety, he answered as calmly as he could muster. "Please do."

Spencer tried not to watch as she gathered his research, but he could not help himself. Phil treated his possessions carefully as she relocated them to the opposite side of the desk. Tiny beads of perspiration popped out at his hairline, but he remained composed, at least on the outside. She retrieved the water basin from the small table, placed it on the desk, opened the bundle, and laid his shave soap and razor on a towel.

"Relax, Spence. All is well."

She stood behind him and ran her hands through his hair. Placing her fingers on his temples, she rubbed slowly in small circles. All Phil had to do was touch him, and he reacted. The effect pacified his sparking nerves, turning his anxiety into immediate arousal.

"There, my dear professor. Be at peace," she whispered.

At her gentle command, he relaxed and rested his head against her ample bosom. He closed his eyes as she spread the shaving soap across his cheeks and chin, savoring her nearness. Her instinct at handling his peculiar anxieties only made him love her more.

The calm atmosphere in the room was heightened by the sound of wood crackling in the hearth and the dogs' slight snores. Her warmth, scent, and the scrape of the blade against his whiskers added to the resonance.

"Promise me you will remain clean-shaven," Phil whispered.

"Perhaps you should stay with me to ensure that I do."

She halted. For a brief moment, he wondered if she would give him a little nick in admonishment, but she continued her task with an exhale. Nor would she acknowledge his statement. Better to remain silent for now. Spencer banished all thoughts from his mind and reveled in the attention. She laid a warm towel on his face, then stepped back.

"Perfect timing. The clock is about to chime twice. Now, why was I summoned to your private lair?" There was a teasing lilt in her voice, and he liked it.

Spencer tossed the towel on the desk and pulled her into his lap. She laughed as she threw her arms about his neck.

"I summoned you because I want you,"—he leaned in and whispered. "I want to make love to you. Right here. Straddle me." He reached into his side pocket and laid two envelopes on his desk. "I planned ahead."

Phil kissed his freshly shaved cheek, lifted her gown, and swung around to face him. "As did I, Spence." She rolled her hips across his erection. "No chemise, corset, or other barriers. I'm naked under this gown." She rubbed against him, causing him to moan with desire.

Together they freed his erect prick and rolled on the sheath. She gazed at him, her brown eyes moist but playful. Spencer held his shaft steady as she took him deep. Phil rocked forward, lifting his hips in concert with her movements. The pace grew frantic, as did their groans of passion. He kissed her, and their tongues met in a fiery clash.

Without any forethought, he stood, holding Phil, still buried deep within. He leaned forward and laid her on the desk. Her hair fanned across the surface like a spilled bottle of red paint. With each driving push, the water basin teetered unsteadily with some sloshing over the sides. A few books fell to the floor. He did not care. Spencer focused on his desire to possess Phil; she was all that mattered, all he yearned for.

Phil writhed, moaning loudly. She completely surrendered to him. He hooked his arms under her knees and plunged deeper, changing the thrust angle. Phil cried out with her release, but he hardly heard it, for he became lost in a mist of flashing colors and lights.

Madness.

But if this is madness, he welcomed and embraced it. He held nothing back as he pounded harder. At last, the colored lights burst into shards as his orgasm slammed him. His back arched, and the cords in his neck pulled tight. When he regained a little semblance of control, he brought Phil to a sitting position and hugged her close.

"My God, Phil. How can you even consider leaving? No matter how far and wide we searched, we would not find this with anyone else."

She stiffened in his embrace and then pushed him away. Blast it. The words slipped out before he had a chance to tamp them down. Embarrassed, Spencer hurriedly put his clothing to rights.

"I cannot be Theodora to your Justinian."

The coolly spoken words sliced his heart in two as cleanly as any sharpened blade.

He stumbled backward and slumped into the chair. "Why ever not?"

She lowered her gown but remained sitting upright, facing him. "That happened hundreds of years ago in another era. Perhaps whore-companions were more accepted then. They are not in this age. Let us say your family, for some unknown reason, accepts me. We're at a dinner, and a corpulent earl waddles into the parlor. Perhaps he is one of my former customers. He calls me out for the harlot I am." Phil exhaled shakily. "Society does not forgive or forget. Not only will you be tainted, but your family will be as well. I will *not* subject you all to such humiliation."

A slow roll of anger passed through him, flaming his insides. "I abhor damned dinners and society, and I'm not acquainted with any corpulent earls! We need never cross their paths," Spencer replied sharply. "And I asked you before not ever to use those words. You are not a whore or a harlot. Not to me, and if they value their lives, not to any in my acquaintance!"

"You must realize you cannot bring your mistress to a family dinner or event. Your father is a duke! A bloody duke! That is one or two steps away from the crown in importance!" Her voice began to rise. Shrill in its emotional fervor.

"What do I care what my father thinks! Who said anything about being my mistress?" he yelled, his emotions bursting through.

"I had considered consenting to be your mistress for an agreed term."

"To the devil with that suggestion! I want you to be my companion. My friend and lover. And when you agree—to marry me."

Phil shook her head vehemently. "No. You *cannot* marry me. It's not to be borne, nor will it be accepted. You *know* this. I have thought this through; the only way is for me to be your mistress. It is the only possible outcome of this impossible and inconceivable situation besides leaving outright." She paused, watching him closely.

Waiting for a reaction? He was so shocked that he was rendered momentarily mute.

"We enjoy each other's company and get on in bed. What more can we ask for?" She continued, her words coming out in a rush. "Being with you this past week has given me insight into the man you are. Honorable and sensitive, but strong and passionate. Yes, and eccentric. I can learn what is forbidden with regard to your possessions and such. We can agree on payment—"

The initial shock was wearing off. Spence stood and grasped her shoulders tight. "Cease this. I never wanted a mistress, and I never will. I lo—"

"No. Please do *not* say the words, or I will shatter into pieces. If you will not consider the mistress route, then I have no other choice. I'm leaving. It is best for us both," she whispered.

The wave of utter devastation that moved through him could not be put into words. "Am I so strange that the thought of sharing my life is abhorrent?" He could not keep the hurt from his voice.

Let her hear it.

Phil cupped his cheeks, meeting his anguished gaze. Her eyes were full of sorrow and regret. "My dear professor. I desire nothing but to share your life; it's why I have to go. In time you will realize I was right."

He grasped her wrists and removed her hands from his face. "You mean to destroy us both with your fright. You're scared witless to feel anything. To reach out and take happiness and hold it in your heart. You would sooner walk away." Spencer pointed toward the door. "Go then. I thought you to be courageous. I was wrong." His voice shook as his eyes grew moist. "Go! I will not stop you!" he yelled.

Phil bolted from the study, slamming the door behind her. Spencer slumped in his chair. A lone tear trailed down his cheek, followed swiftly by another.

For the first time in his life, he allowed himself to feel.

All because of Phil.

It turns out, he should have stayed in his protective shell where no one or nothing could hurt him. He took a chance on love, and it detonated his heart and soul into a pile of smoldering ash.

Chapter 22

THE REST OF THE AFTERNOON passed by with a numbing blur. Phil lay on the bed in her room, alternately crying or cursing as the sun set. Spence had left her alone the rest of the day. Did she honestly expect him to seek her out after that heated and impassioned argument?

The professor certainly did not remain quiet. Doors slammed, and his heavy tread could be heard on the stairs more than once. Perhaps he'd taken the dogs for a walk. Regardless, she decided not to leave her room or even prepare supper. Nausea had killed her appetite.

Phil *knew* their time together would end with high words and overwrought emotions. Bloody hell—he'd nearly declared his love for her. Why couldn't he understand that what she did and said was for his benefit more than hers? She loved him enough to protect him from the life he would have had if she had stayed with him.

Oh, how she hurt.

Her insides roiled as wave after wave of queasiness clutched her tight. Alone in the darkened room, she wondered if she had made the correct decision. Spence called her a coward —and he had the right of it. She was scared sick. It wasn't supposed to transpire like this. The plan was for her to remain impartial and emotionally removed from the paid task.

How and when had it all gone wrong?

The answer? The first time she met him.

He captivated her in all ways. The potent mixture of virile male and discernible vulnerability touched her deep in a part of her soul she thought long dead. With a sigh, she pulled the quilt over her, trying to stay warm.

Those complicated feelings grew with each roll and pitch of his rich, baritone voice, gentle touch, and caring actions. Never mind his lovemaking only increased in depth and significance each time they joined. She moaned softly as she recalled how he laid her on his desk only a few hours ago and rogered her quite masterfully. Weariness claimed her, and she drifted to sleep as the tears dried on her cheeks.

PHIL AWOKE WITH A START. She lay in complete blackness. Her stomach grumbled, reminding her she had not eaten since breakfast. After fumbling for the matches on the end table, she struck one and lit the candle. Holding it aloft, she scanned the room. The ancient clock on the wall read fifteen minutes past seven.

She pulled the gown over her head and laid it at the end of the bed. She should have removed it before she fell asleep. Phil reached for the nightshirt. Before putting it on, she raised it to her nose and inhaled. Spence's faint scent was still present. The odor of cloves and pine filled her nostrils. Poking her arms through the holes of the garment, she strode toward the door. No sound. She slipped into the hall and padded down the stairs as quietly as a mouse.

AFTER THE SHOCK OF Phil's rejection had somewhat worn off, Spencer managed to keep busy with several mundane tasks. Whom was he kidding? The shock may never wear off. It left a deep scar on his heart and soul—permanent damage, to be certain.

He brought wood in from outside, then walked the dogs and fed them. He packed up more of his books and research. He even washed items of clothing and packed part of his trunk. There was no chance he would stay here now. How could he ever sit at that desk again and try to work without thinking of Phil spread across it, passionately thrashing about?

He lay on his bed in the darkness, trying to understand what had happened. What more could he possibly say to convince her to stay? He said all he could physically, he tried to convey it verbally, but she wouldn't have it.

In a week, Spencer went from a green lad to a man of seduction he did not even recognize. Perhaps the passionate nature lay deeply hidden, the trait common with his family members. His brothers certainly enjoyed sexual activity. He knew his parents loved each other. Why couldn't he be capable of feeling the same, different as he is?

Phil was the one who set the complicated emotions free. Her experience with men, though lengthy in years, didn't have much depth to it. The vain thought that he was the only man to bring out her most passionate feelings lingered. He hadn't imagined her emotional response.

They were given an extraordinary gift of ardent love and respectful companionability he knew instinctively to be rare. They did not have to be alone anymore or hide their emotions. A private world all their own.

They could have it all.

But Spencer also acknowledged his "other" nature, which spoke of a peculiar man with eccentric habits and strange ways. Who barely had control over the emotions that lay under his atypical way of dealing with life? The internal struggle would remain with him until the end of his days. Did he want to subject the woman he loved more than anything to such a life state?

Perhaps he *should* say goodbye and protect her from him and his outlandish habits and reactions.

Or he should cease ruminating over this entirely. This was how Spencer dealt with situations beyond the norm, by repeatedly working through the conundrum until he reached a satisfactory conclusion.

A slight noise outside his door pulled him from his thoughts. One of the dogs? After several minutes he rose and walked to the door. Opening it, he gazed into the darkened hall and listened for movement. Nothing, perhaps he imagined it. About to close the door, the toe of his boot hit something solid.

Spencer bent down and picked up the tray. Phil had brought him a dinner of ham, potatoes, and green beans with a couple of slices of bread and a sprig of grapes. After taking two steps into the hall, he stopped. A decided warmth curled about his heart. He may have one last opportunity to make his case for their mutual happiness. He must try. His very life depended on it. And Phil deserved to find joy in her life.

Was leaving her the only solution? He loved her enough to let her go.

Even if it would destroy him.

FOR PHIL, SLEEP DID not come easy the previous night. In fact, she watched the sun rise. After packing her meager belongings, she changed into the green gown she'd arrived in. Except now, it was a torn and greasy mess. Cleaning a filthy kitchen and falling off a cliff would do that to a dress. Thankfully, her wool coat covered most of the damage. It would have to suffice.

Should she stay hidden in this room until Boyle and his cart make an appearance? What if the old grocer didn't come today? She could not bear staying here with Spence any longer. It hurt too much. Although Phil's resolve crumbled quite a bit during the long night hours, it would not take much for the rest of the wall of denial to tumble down. If he asked her to stay, there was a good chance she would rush to his arms and happily acquiesce.

She reached for both carpetbags with a heavy heart and stepped toward the door. Phil halted as she found it hard to catch her breath. Her booted feet would not move forward. A giant sob escaped her mouth as she dropped the bags. They hit the floor with a dull thud.

Scanning her surroundings, Phil found she no longer stood in a musty, dusty room in a long-neglected hunting lodge. In her mind's eye, it transformed into an enchanted castle, and its magical aura smashed the last bit of her stubborn defenses. Inside the castle lived a prince with a noble and passionate heart. One that, beyond all reason, loved her and wished to share his life with her. Love, in all its complicated but compelling splendor.

What a fool. How could she even consider departing?

She loved Spence too much to leave him. For all her supposed brave talk of sparing him future heartbreak, the truth of the situation could not be denied. Phil could not bear to smash his heart to bits. Nor hers. Nor could she deny the love that they shared. In such a brief period? Logic would scoff at such a predicament. Never mind their divergent backgrounds.

Against all odds, love bloomed between them. Another ragged cry left her throat as tears spilled down her cheeks. In the face of love, one that she desperately tried to deny, her remaining lingering doubts dissipated into nothingness. Instead, she embraced love fully. And it filled her with such delight that Phil thought her heart would burst.

A knock sounded at the door.

"May I come in?"

Phil cleared her throat and wiped the moisture from her face with the sleeve of her coat. "Yes."

Spence looked entirely handsome in his black trousers and white shirt. It lay open at the neck, showing an enticing peek at the brown hair on his chest. His expression was guarded, but judging by the dark circles under his eyes, he didn't sleep either.

"Ready to leave, I see. Even have your coat on. Are you that anxious to be shunt of me?" His voice was quiet; hurt laced his tone.

More tears threatened, and her hands shook. Phil tried to speak but could not. If she answered him, she would fall to pieces and lose all control. Instead, she shook her head.

Spence clasped his hands behind his back. "I'm aware that I am not a woman's dream mate. I'm hardly an adventurer or a taker of risks. Nor am I a rake with vast sexual and seductive experience. I'd rather research those attributes in others. I've been called dull, boring, and odd. Perhaps I am. But I ask you not to leave." He paused, and she met his gaze. His lovely eyes burned with passion and feeling.

"You have become such a part of my life in such a short span," he continued. "How can I go on without you? Who will see I eat regularly? Make me toast and cheese by the fire? See that I shave? Who will—love me?" Spence stepped closer.

Phil choked back a sob, her trembling hand covering her mouth.

"Be my Theodora. Work and live at my side until the end of our days. I love you beyond all description. Beyond all-knowing. When you're ready, I want us to marry, to commit to each other. You are my first and my last. Give me life. Give me love."

Tears streamed down her cheeks as she ran to his arms. "Bloody hell, yes!" Phil cried. "I love you more than I ever imagined possible, Spence. I tried to deny it, but I could not. Not any longer. I'm yours, my dearest Justinian."

He laughed and spun her around. The dogs—who had followed Spence in—barked happily.

"Then you will come with me to Penhaven? As soon as we can arrange it?" Spence asked hopefully.

She nodded. "Yes. Oh, yes."

Spence cupped her cheeks, giving her such a tender yet passionate look that she melted. Then he captured her lips with his, kissing her deeply, thoroughly, and weakening her knees. How she loved his kisses. How she loved him.

The road ahead held an uncertainty that thrilled and frightened her, but the professor and the prostitute would meet the challenges head-on.

Love can give you courage. Give you hope. Together they would make their own path. And bask in the joy of loving.

Epilogue

THE JOURNEY TO PENHAVEN took about a week, but Spencer didn't mind as long as Phil was by his side. Boyle arrived that afternoon, and Spencer returned with him to the nearby village. After acquiring horses, a carriage, a driver, and other supplies, he returned to Phil early the next morning, and they spent the next two days packing.

Everything after that was a whirlwind of activity. They stopped in London long enough for Phil to make specific provisions at the Starling Club. Eventually, she would sell it, but for now, she left Darius Brownlow in charge. Spencer would never presume to interfere, what she wanted to do regarding her business was entirely her decision, and he would support her in whatever she arranged.

Phil was curled up in his arms, napping. That this splendid woman loved him—humbled him and had him in complete awe. Having this for a lifetime was more than he could comprehend.

On the opposite seat, Theodora was asleep, with Justinian lying on a blanket on the carriage floor. While in London, Spencer sent word to his small staff at Penhaven to ready the house for their imminent arrival. Thomas Wheeler, the driver he had hired, was a jack of all trades and a pleasant man of middling years. He would make him his valet once they arrived, as he'd indicated he would be interested in a permanent position.

The carriage turned up the hill toward his small estate. Spencer kissed Phil's cheek. "Awake, my love. We are nearly there."

She yawned, then pulled the curtains aside. Winter sunshine poured into the carriage. "Not as much snow here. There's a mercy."

Spencer chuckled. "But nearly as isolated. Though the town is not far."

Phil smiled warmly. "I don't mind a bit." The gray brick manor house came into view. "Oh, it's larger than I imagined. How rich are you?"

"Wealthy enough for us all to live comfortably the rest of our lives."

Justinian woofed in agreement.

"Bloody hell, how many servants?" Phil marveled.

The carriage pulled up to the front entrance, and four men and three women, all in livery or maid's attire, lined up outside. "Seven, for now. We will have to hire quite a few more. As the lady of the house, the duty falls to you if you wish."

"I do. I'm skilled at picking the right people for a job."

He caressed her cheek with the tip of his finger. "That you are, my love."

The carriage door opened. "Welcome home, my lord."

Spencer stepped out, turned, and held out his hand for Phil. They managed to buy her various garments for the trip, with more to be delivered. He was actually sorry to see the green-striped gown go. He wanted to lavish all sorts of gifts on her, but Phil gently suggested that he rein in his impulses, at least for now.

"Garrison. Good to see you. This is Miss Philomena McGrattan. My fiancée."

"A pleasure, miss."

They were going to marry.

When, however, hadn't been decided. Spencer left it up to Phil. She mentioned later in the spring, and he was fine with that. At some point, he would have to introduce her to the family, but until then, all he wanted was for them to be alone—or at least as alone as one could be on an estate employed with various servants.

As they entered the hall, the wolfhounds following behind, Garrison said, "My lord, you wanted me to inform you when you received word from your family. Letters are awaiting you in your study. I will leave your trunk in your room for you to unpack."

His staff knew him well —and his various quirks. "Very good. The coachman, Thomas Wheeler. See him settled. He will be my valet going forward. Give him your wise guidance. In the meantime, bring tea and sandwiches, will you?" He would have to adjust to Wheeler being his valet. Spencer would ensure the transition moved ahead in a slow and deliberate fashion.

"Right away, my lord. And I will see to Mr. Wheeler."

Phil removed her cloak and turned in a circle, taking in his study. "It's very much you. Books everywhere."

Spencer picked up the letters. Two from his parents. One from Harrison. Another from Tremain. Didn't expect that.

Phil leaned in, glancing at the envelope. "Who is The Reverend T. Colson? And where is Hawksgreen?"

"In Kent. And this letter is from Tremain, my brother."

"He's a vicar? I thought he was a soldier?"

"Tremain's story is—complicated."

"I'd love to hear it over tea. Why not sit by the fire and read the letter? I'll pour once the tray arrives."

Phil instinctively understood what he wanted; it was one of the many reasons he loved her. Spence sat in his leather chair and ripped open the envelope.

DEAR SPENCE,

I know you are probably still in Wales, but I sent this to Penhaven because there is no need for a speedy reply, if one at all. But I have to tell my feelings to someone.

I am not certain I can continue with this. I've become a brooding bastard. It must be bad if even I acknowledge it. And because of it, I've become ineffective regarding my duties. Perhaps this has all been a mistake. It would be easy to escape to Gransford Manor, but then I remembered what I told you when we were at school. Hold your head high, and don't show fear. I have found it is easier said than done.

I know you are not one for letter writing, but drop me a line during some break in your research, for I need your sage advice. I am not sure what to do next.

I am lost, Brother.

Love,

Tremain

SPENCER FOLDED THE letter. Tremain was the most gregarious and carefree of the three brothers until the war. For him to write this showed he was in crisis. What could Spencer do?

Offer his love and support. Immediately.

What could he say? He gripped the envelope tightly, and it crinkled under the pressure.

"I have to reply to this."

Phil held out her hand. "And you will. But first, come and sit. Tea will be here directly. Relax, have a bite to eat, then you will be rested and refreshed and more able to craft a suitable response."

What would he do without her? Her soft words eased his tension. He took her hand, leaned down, and kissed her forehead. "I love you."

His life, at last, was complete. How he wished the same for his dear brothers.

~~~SEE A SNEAK PREVIEW of Tremain's story, *The Vicar's Frozen Heart*, further along.

More Books by Karyn Gerrard

~HISTORICAL~

The Spinster and Mr. Glover (Book #1 Blind Cupid Series)

The Governess and the Beast (Book #2 Blind Cupid Series)

The Copper and the Madam (Book #3 Blind Cupid Series)

Protecting the Duke (The Rakes of St. Regent's Park #1)

The Baron and the Mistress (The Rakes of St. Regent's Park #2)

Bold Seduction (Of Professor Hornsby) (Book #1 Hornsby Brothers Series)

The Vicar's Frozen Heart (Book #2 Hornsby Brothers Series)

Marquess of Secrets (Book #3 Hornsby Brothers Series)

Beloved Monster (Book #1 The Ravenswood Chronicles)

Beloved Beast (Book #2 The Ravenswood Chronicles)

Marriage with a Proper Stranger (Book #1 Men of Wollstonecraft Hall Series)

Scandal with a Sinful Scot (Book #2 Men of Wollstonecraft Hall Series)

Love with a Notorious Rake (Book #3 Men of Wollstonecraft Hall Series)

Knight of Christmas (The Rakes of St. Regent's Park #3)

The Duke of Pain (The Rakes of St. Regent's Park #4)

The Not So Perfect Duke (The Rakes of St. Regent's Park #5)

~CONTEMPORARY~

My Highlander Cover Model (Heroes of Time Travel Anthology Series #1)

Timeless Heart (Heroes of Time Travel Anthology Series #2)

That Christmas Feeling (It's Never Too Late for Love Anthology Series #2)

My Wicked Soul (It's Never Too Late for Love Anthology Series #1)

Wild Pitch

He's the Wicked Bad (Wicked Men of Rockland City #1)

His Wicked Celtic Kiss (Wicked Men of Rockland City #2)

Author Biography

A MULTI-PUBLISHED AUTHOR from Eastern Canada, Karyn Gerrard loves to write sensual historical and contemporary romances. Tortured heroes are an absolute must.

Karyn's been happily married for a long time to her own hero. His encouragement and loving support keep her moving forward.

To learn more about Karyn and her books, visit www.karyngerrard.com[1]

Also, visit her on Facebook, Twitter, Pinterest, Instagram, and Bookbub.

"LOOKING FOR A SWOON-worthy read? You can't go wrong with the lovely and emotional romances from Karyn Gerrard." ~**Vanessa Kelly, USA Today Bestselling author**

"Karyn Gerrard writes very enjoyable, richly textured historical romances." ~**Kate Pearce, New York Times and USA Today Bestselling author**

---

1.   http://www.karyngerrard.com/

Sneak Peek of The Vicar's Frozen Heart

Book #2 (Hornsby Brothers) by Karyn Gerrard

Chapter 1

JANUARY 1882
Yorkshire, England

DURING HER SHORT LIFE, Eliza Winston had been reprimanded more than once for her bluntness and impulsive actions. Still, she'd never experienced a dressing down quite as vicious as the one Lady Bowater was giving her. Standing in the drawing room with the housekeeper, Mrs. Travers, Eliza faced the firing squad with her head held high. But inside? Her emotions were in turmoil.

"I will not tolerate this sort of loose morals in any member of my staff, Miss Winston. Especially *not* in a governess," Lady Bowater huffed. "Do you deny you've had carnal relations with my son?"

"I do not deny it. If you ask William, my lady, he will inform you the consensual assignation was of a brief duration." Eliza's voice shook at the last words.

Their affair had lasted ten days, culminating with two mediocre tumbles between the sheets. Well, perhaps more than passable, as she had limited experience. None at all if the truth were told.

"He's Mr. Winters to you, my girl!" Mrs. Travers snapped.

Lady Bowater held up her hand to silence the housekeeper. "I've spoken with my son, and he claims that he's formed an attachment to you. It will not be borne. He's agreed that the time has come for a stint in the army. It will do him a world of good. Build character. Quite a shame we cannot do the same with you."

Eliza winced inwardly.

Poor William.

"You've worked here two years, and I am extremely disappointed that my trust in you has been sorely misplaced. You're dismissed effective immediately." Mrs. Travers bobbed her head in agreement at Lady Bowater's admonishing tone. "You will be given twenty pounds, but I *will* have assurances you will not turn up on this doorstep again, even if you find yourself with child. Those are the conditions."

It sounded as if Lady Bowater had done this before. Eliza would not be surprised as William had two older brothers.

Wait. Twenty pounds? A year's wages?

The large amount was to ensure that she would keep quiet in case there were consequences to the liaison. There would be no child. With knowledge comes power, and Eliza had insisted that William wore sheaths, though there was no absolute guarantee. Notwithstanding, she gave her ladyship a stiff nod in agreement.

Eliza clasped her hands to stem the shaking. Despite her brave front, inside, she was crumbling into pieces. Her heart ached with regret—and shame.

"Mrs. Travers has written you a letter of reference. It's adequate for your needs." The housekeeper thrust an envelope into Eliza's hand. "Your trunk has been packed and brought downstairs. Furthermore, I've arranged transport to take you far from this estate and Yorkshire."

"My lady, why provide transportation?" Eliza didn't like the sound of this. "A carriage ride to the nearest train would be tolerable enough."

Lady Bowater took a step toward her. "I want you off the property immediately. If you are waiting about for the trains, William could find you. He is young and impulsive."

Goodness, Lady Bowater was not wasting a moment. It indeed appeared as if she'd done this before. Undoubtedly, there were many scenes with the older sons over the years.

"It's seven o'clock, my lady. Couldn't my departure wait until morning?" Eliza asked, her voice shaking on the last two words as the reality of what was happening took hold.

"No. For the exact reason I've stated. There is to be no further contact between you and my son. I want you gone—before he discovers your absence. There's been enough drama for my liking."

Lady Bowater handed an envelope to Mrs. Travers, who in turn passed it to Eliza, repulsion evident on both their faces. Eliza's heart tumbled, the ramifications of her brief dalliance hitting hard. She had managed to secure a good position through sheer determination—and now it was ruined.

All on me.

For the specific reason that she should have shown forbearance in the face of a tempting rendezvous. She was more intelligent than that. At least, she had thought so. What a colossal blunder. All she had to do was say no. Be strong and resolute.

"My men will escort you through the night to Dover. The farther you are from here, the better."

"Dover?" Eliza blinked rapidly. "My lady, wouldn't travel by train the entire distance be more expedient?"

"I don't trust you. You could disembark at any stop. I want you delivered personally to the Southeast Coast," Lady Bowater answered haughtily. "However, I gave my men permission to use the train part of the way should the weather deteriorate."

Eliza gulped. "But I've never been to Southeast England. I don't know anyone—"

"Exactly. Begone from my sight. Vixen." Lady Bowater's face flushed with self-righteous anger or abhorrence, maybe both, as Eliza couldn't be sure. Dramatic words from a woman who claimed to abhor drama.

It sounds like a line from an overwrought play.

Eliza wasn't sure whether to laugh or cry.

Lady Bowater's eyes narrowed. "Seducer of innocent boys."

Boy?

Granted, pretty William was four years her junior, but he was certainly old enough for an illicit encounter at twenty years of age. And hardly all that innocent, as he appeared to know what he was about in bed. Nevertheless, the words hit their mark, churning her insides.

Mrs. Travers clasped Eliza's elbow tightly and steered her from the room. "A fine mess you've got yourself in, my girl. All to have a young lordling in your bed. Stupid, stupid," Mrs. Travers whispered fiercely as she pulled her toward the downstairs entrance.

She wriggled out of the housekeeper's clutches. "One moment, please. Allow me to inspect my room one last time and collect my coat and reticule. At least grant me that."

Sighing, Mrs. Travers did an about-face and pulled Eliza upstairs toward the servants' quarters. For an older lady, she could move quickly. An enormous ring of keys bounced against her hip with each long stride. Mrs. Travers stopped in front of the door and released her. Frowning, Eliza rubbed her arm. Thanks to the housekeeper's tight grip, there will no doubt be bruises.

"Make haste," Mrs. Travers ordered. "I'll wait here."

After slipping into the room, Eliza closed the door and leaned against it. Tears welled in her eyes the instant she found herself alone.

What have I done?

She'd made a complete muck of things. With no family to turn to, what could she do?

Dover. Good heavens.

She didn't have to stay in the immediate vicinity; she could travel anywhere with twenty pounds. The money and reference would be lost if she refused to follow Lady Bowater's demand. It would be best to make a swift and quiet exit. Perhaps a fresh start on the opposite end of the country *was* prudent.

Blinking away the tears, she sniffled while glancing about the room. She loved her living space. It was bright and pleasant, with a comfortable bed and a large window to let in the sunlight. Better accommodations than at the orphanage. It had become—home. Or what she imagined home was.

During the past two years, Eliza had added little touches to make the room her own, a rug, a framed picture of a calm ocean, and a blue quilt with a star design. The items weren't here; hopefully, they were placed in her trunk and not tossed in the rubbish bin. Inspecting all the drawers and seeing that nothing was left behind, Eliza spied her shawl on a wall hook. She pulled it down, opened the envelope, and carefully separated the pound notes, tucking a few in each of the shawl's hidden pockets.

When traveling with money, hiding it on your person was the sensible thing to do. The wool coat must be with her trunk. Standing in the middle of the room, a tug of regret filled her. How she would miss Lady Susanna, her delightful young charge. They wouldn't even allow her to say goodbye.

A right mess, indeed.

Curiosity and a spark of passion caused her to throw away her hard-won position and security.

Eliza grew up at the St. Ann's Industrial School and Orphanage and studied to be a governess, a respected position within the pecking order of the servant world. Not an easy situation to obtain, but she had accomplished it. Only to abandon it as soon as William's lips touched hers. Perhaps she *was* a vixen. No, she was lonely and had been her whole life. That is why she tossed all common sense to the wind.

Too late for regrets.

A brave face is what was needed for this sorry situation. She would depart this estate as calmly as she could. Like it or not, it was time to move on with the rest of her life.

ELIZA COULD NOT SAY how many hours had passed. The rocking of the carriage made sleep impossible. Instead, she recalled the humiliating scolding she'd received. How arrogant of her to think she could indulge in a clandestine relationship with the earl's youngest son. His handsome face, golden hair, and broad shoulders awakened something inside her. A passion she had no inkling existed.

Such intimacy.

Perhaps William sensed her desperation for warmth and human contact. Somehow, she doubted the young man was aware of another's loneliness.

Rubbing her burning, tired eyes, Eliza pushed aside the curtain and glanced outside. Complete blackness filled the horizon except for the snow tumbling from the sky. The snow looked to be rather deep. Considering it was the middle of January, a clear road for passage was too much to ask. With a sudden jolt, the carriage came to a halt.

One of the men clamored down and opened the door. "'Tis cold ridin' up there. Thought I'd get a wee bit of warmth from ye, lassie."

Even in dark shadows, there was no mistaking the lascivious look on the older man's face.

Oh, no.

"Where are we? What's the time—wait, what are you doing?" Eliza cried.

He pushed his way into the carriage, slammed the door, and banged on the roof. The carriage lurched forward, slowly at first, as if struggling to push through the snow. Unpleasant sweat, whiskey, and cheap pipe tobacco odors filled the interior. A horrible scar pulled the man's mouth into a sadistic leer.

"I searched your trunk up top. No money. Give over, lass. Where 'tis it? Don't be lyin' to me. I heard the whole sorry tale in the servant's dinin' hall. I know the old hag gave ye money." He snatched the reticule from her wrist with a rough tug, snapping the straps. He looked inside, frowned, and tossed it to the floor. Grunting, he pushed her down and lay on top of her, his large hands running up and down her body. Then he crammed them in her coat, searching her pockets.

Eliza shuddered with horror when the man's growing erection pressed against her thigh.

"Give it over, or I'll take the amount out of your cunny. His young lordship left ye well oiled; I'll be bound," he hissed in her ear. "You're not the first nor the last. Those Winter boys like their fun. They won't mind if I take their leavings."

A hand closed about her throat, the callous tips of his fingers scraping her skin. Scar leaned in, his foul breath turning her stomach. "Give it to me, or I'll hump the truth from ye." His other hand fumbled with the fall of his trousers.

No. No. No!

Frantically, Eliza pulled off one of her wool gloves with her teeth, then raked her nails over his eye and down his cheek. Scar screamed, releasing his hold. Scrambling backward, he buried his face in his hands, droplets of blood oozing between his meaty fingers.

The driver must have heard his partner's screech, for the carriage slowed slightly. Turning, she fumbled with the door handle.

Escape!

Eliza's heart banged against her ribs at a frightening pace. Scar recovered quickly, grabbing her arm and wrenching her shoulder, then he smashed his clenched fist into her face. Bone cracked, and blood trickled over her lips.

A jolt of intense pain spiraled through her, causing her vision to blur, but she finally grasped the handle and gave it a turn, causing the door to fling open wide. The carriage was still moving.

Jump!

What choice did she have? About to lunge forward, Scar caught a fistful of her shawl and pulled her back in. Blindly she fought him; her breathing labored, landing blows where she could. He swore obscenely and shook her hard. In the fracas, her shawl came off.

The money!

Eliza desperately grabbed it, but Scar shoved her, and she tumbled backward out of the swaying carriage. Hitting the ground hard, she rolled and rolled, gathering cold snow until she came to a halt in a ditch. Searing pain covered her entire body.

"Whoa, there!" the driver called out. Drifting in and out of consciousness, she heard snippets of conversation and raised voices wafting in the cold night air.

"What did ye do, ye great lummox! Ye were to get the money, nothing else."

"Bitch fought me. She rolled down a hill, probably dead."

"Be damned if I be checking. It was an accident, not our fault. Her ladyship never needs to know. Not that she'd care much. Throw the trunk off and—"

"Look, here 'tis. Hidden in her shawl. Aye, let's ditch the trunk and head to London. I could do with a pint and a slice of kidney pie."

More chatter, sprinkled with smug laughter. They were going to leave her here to freeze to death. Eliza lay perfectly still in case they returned to do further investigating. Satisfied with finding the money—*oh, my money*—she heard the trunk hit the ground with a decided thud. With a snap of the reins, the men drove off.

Snowflakes gathered on her lashes. Could she stand? No. Instead, Eliza tried to crawl. Could it be a house she'd spotted amongst the trees, or was her scrambled mind playing tricks? Tasting blood, she pulled herself through the snow. A white-hot stab of pain shot through her head, and everything turned black.

SINCE SWEARING OFF laudanum, Tremain Colson had become a fitful sleeper. The incessant pain in his leg often woke him several times during the night. After lighting the wick in the oil lamp beside his bed, he glanced at the wall clock—half past four in the morning.

What sort of racket awoke him? The whinny of horses—and men's voices raised in excitement and anger. What brain-addled individuals would be traveling this time of night and in inclement weather? There was also a loud thump, as though something had been tossed to the ground.

The temptation to roll over and ignore the clamor had crossed his mind, but something kept nudging him to investigate. That thudding sound could be a human, and no one could survive long in these stormy conditions.

With an exasperated sigh, Tremain swung his legs around the side of the bed and sat upright, rubbing his eyes and grunting at the twinge that shot up his right limb. He pushed himself into a standing position, then limped to his small wardrobe and dressed swiftly. Clasping his cane, he ventured into the darkened hallway, located a lamp, and lit it. After slipping on his wool greatcoat and gloves, he wrapped a thick scarf around his head and face, then headed outside. A blast of icy wind slammed into him, seizing his breath.

Holding the light aloft, Tremain cautiously ventured across his property. A large trunk lay in a drift of snow. The deep ruts left behind by a carriage were already filling in. Snow swirled all about him as the wind howled with a woeful wail. Turning in a circle, he looked about. Nothing but white as far as the eye could see. And dark sky. His gaze skirted across a large mound. There in the ditch, a bare hand lay exposed.

Tremain tottered toward the trench, taking his time as the ground inclined downward. Sitting the lantern and his cane at his feet, he swiped away the loose snow.

An unconscious woman.